AMBUSH!

The yipping and howling grew to a crescendo.

Facing straight ahead, Fargo came to the far side of the thicket. He was moving so fast, he didn't see a man coming the other way until they were right on top of one another. They both halted in their tracks.

It was hard to say which one of them was more surprised, Fargo or the Apache returning to camp, his arms laden with firewood. But the Apache reacted first. Dropping the branches, he swooped forward like a bird of prey. . . .

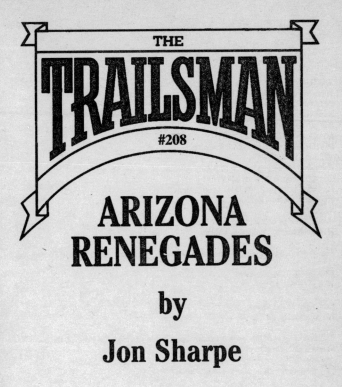

THE TRAILSMAN

#208

ARIZONA RENEGADES

by

Jon Sharpe

A SIGNET BOOK

SIGNET
Published by the Penguin Group
Penguin Putnam Inc., 375 Hudson Street,
New York, New York 10014, U.S.A.
Penguin Books Ltd, 27 Wrights Lane,
London W8 5TZ, England
Penguin Books Australia Ltd, Ringwood,
Victoria, Australia
Penguin Books Canada Ltd, 10 Alcorn Avenue,
Toronto, Ontario, Canada M4V 3B2
Penguin Books (N.Z.) Ltd, 182–190 Wairau Road,
Auckland 10, New Zealand

Penguin Books Ltd, Registered Offices:
Harmondsworth, Middlesex, England

First published by Signet, an imprint of Dutton NAL, a member of Penguin Putnam Inc.

First Printing, March, 1999
10 9 8 7 6 5 4 3 2 1

The first chapter of this book originally appeared in *Chimney Rock Burial,* the two
hundred and seventh volume in this series.

Ⓤ REGISTERED TRADEMARK—MARCA REGISTRADA

Printed in the United States of America

The Trailsman

Beginnings . . . they bend the tree and they mark the man. Skye Fargo was born when he was eighteen. Terror was his midwife, vengeance his first cry. Killing spawned Skye Fargo, ruthless, cold-blooded murder. Out of the acrid smoke of gunpowder still hanging in the air, he rose, cried out a promise never forgotten.

The Trailsman they began to call him all across the West: searcher, scout, hunter, the man who could see where others only looked, his skills for hire but not his soul, the man who lived each day to the fullest, yet trailed each tomorrow. Skye Fargo, the Trailsman, and the seeker who could take the wildness of a land and the wanting of a woman and make them his own.

1861—a baked hellhole soon to be known
as the Arizona Territory, where hatred,
greed, and bloodlust cost
countless lives. . . .

1

Apaches had been stalking the big man in buckskins for half an hour.

Most men would not have realized it. For a typical townsman or settler, the day was ideal for travel. Scattered clouds floated lazily in a vivid blue sky, wafted by a warm breeze from the southwest. The same breeze stirred the grama grass so it rippled like waves on an ocean. Here and there yucca trees poked skyward like small islands.

The countryside was picturesque and peaceful but the big man on the pinto wasn't fooled by appearance. It was too peaceful, too quiet. Birds should be singing. Rabbits and lizards, usually so plentiful, were nowhere to be seen. Except for the rustling of the grass, the only sounds were the clomp of the Ovaro's hooves and the creak of saddle leather.

Skye Fargo shifted to scan the gently rolling country on both sides of the rutted dirt road he followed. His piercing lake blue eyes narrowed when he spotted grass that bent much further than it should. His ears pricked at the scrape of a knee on earth, a sound so faint no townsman or settler would have heard it.

Fargo's senses were not like those of most men. Years of living in the wild had honed them to the razor edge of a bowie. His eyes were the eyes of a hawk, his ears those of a mountain lion, his nose that of a coyote. He saw and heard and smelled things not one man in a hundred would notice. It was part of the reason others called him the Trailsman, the reason why he was widely regarded as one of the best scouts alive. Put simply, his wilderness savvy was second to none.

Fargo pretended not to see the grass bend, pretended he had not heard the knee scrape. He didn't want those who were stalking him to know he knew they were there. Acting as innocent as a newborn babe, he pretended to yawn while stretching to give them the notion he was much more tired than he was. When he lowered his right hand to his hip, he contrived to place it next to the smooth butt of the Colt strapped around his lean waist. His broad shoulders swiveled as he scoured the road ahead for the likeliest spot for the attack. The Apaches would strike soon. He was within seven or eight miles of the San Simon River and the stage station on its east bank.

Personally, Fargo would be glad to get there. The most dangerous part of his journey would be over. He had done as he promised, and once he crossed the San Simon, he could get on with his own affairs. Maybe head for San Antonio, and from there north to Denver to look up an old friend. The thought of her silken hair and lush body brought a smile to his dry lips. A smile that turned into a scowl of annoyance for letting his mind drift at the worst possible moment. He must stay alert or he would pay for his folly with his life.

Apaches rarely made mistakes. They were fierce fighters, proud and independent. Of late their attacks had grown more frequent, more savage, as they struggled to resist the white tide washing over their land.

Until five or six months ago things had been relatively quiet. Except for an occasional raid on a ranch or way station, the Apaches had been content to stay in their mountain retreats. Then all hell busted loose. Rumor had it a new leader was to blame. A young hothead who went by the name of Chipota was stirring the tribes up, saying the only way to rid their land of the hated whites was to unite. To rise up as one and drive their enemies out in the greatest bloodbath in Apache history.

Up ahead a knoll appeared. Fargo stayed in the middle of

the road so he would have a split-second warning should warriors rush from either side. Not many were stalking him. The two he had pinpointed, possibly a couple more.

That the Apaches had shadowed him for so long without doing anything was somewhat surprising. Fargo had passed several likely spots for an ambush, yet they never jumped him. He reckoned they were up to one of their notorious tricks, that they had something special in mind which would guarantee success. His life depended on figuring out what that trick was.

Apaches were supremely wary by nature. They never took needless chances, never ran the risk of losing one of their own if it could be avoided. From infancy, Apache males were rigorously schooled in the Apache virtues of killing without being killed and stealing without being caught. This creed was everything to them, the code, as it were, on which their whole lives were based.

The open ground worked in Fargo's favor. There were no boulders for Apaches to hide behind, no ravines or clefts in which to secrete themselves. The only cover was the grama grass—but that was enough where Apaches were concerned. They were masters at blending into the background, at appearing as part of any landscape. Apaches could literally hide in plain sight.

Fargo arched his back as if he had a kink in it, when really he wanted to rise a little higher so he could probe the grass bordering the knoll. The top was barren, worn by wind as well as the passage of countless horses, oxen, and mules.

The Ovaro suddenly pricked its ears and nickered. Fargo had no idea why. The road was empty, and there was nowhere on the barren knoll for Apaches to hide. He wondered if the pinto had caught the scent of a warrior lurking in the grass.

Fargo firmed his grip on the Colt but didn't draw. Doing so would let the Apaches know he was on to them. Crazy as it sounded, Fargo *wanted* them to spring their ambush. He would rather they tried to make buzzard bait of him than a family of unsuspecting pilgrims or merchants freighting goods. The average traveler didn't stand a prayer. Which was why army patrols were so frequent, or had been until just recently.

At the base of the knoll the Ovaro abruptly snorted and shied. Fargo had to goad it on, his puzzlement growing since he still saw nothing to account for it. The warrior he'd heard earlier was off to the left and slightly to the rear. Another Apache was on the right, maybe forty feet out. Neither showed any inclination to venture nearer. Why, then, was the Ovaro so bothered?

Fargo started up the gentle slope. Countless wheels had worn deep ruts. Countless hooves had hammered the earth until it was hard-packed. To the north a red hawk wheeled high in the sky. To the east rising plumes of dust caught Fargo's eye and he swore under his breath. Riders or a wagon were approaching. The Apaches must already know. Maybe they were lying low because they wanted to take more lives than that of a lone horseman.

Troubled, Fargo reined up. He had an urge to pull his hat brim low against the harsh sun but he didn't take his hand off the Colt. Another check of the grama grass was unrewarding. Mulling whether to hurry on and warn whoever was approaching, he idly glanced at the ground, at a patch of earth near the road's edge. Something about it spiked his interest although at first he could not say what it was. The ground looked *different,* somehow. Fargo glanced away, then gazed at it again. Yes, the soil had definitely been disturbed. It was looser, small clumps proof it had been freshly churned, possibly by Apache mounts.

However, when Fargo peered intently at the spot, no hoofprints were evident. There were none at all. Which was odd since tracks were everywhere else. It was as if the earth had been wiped clean, just like a schoolboy's slate.

Fargo noticed the size and shape of the disturbed soil. An area roughly six feet long and three feet wide. Then he noticed something else, his breath catching in his throat. Jutting from the ground, not more than a fingernail high, was what appeared to be the stump of a weed that had taken root. Only it was circular and hollow and more closely resembled a *reed* than a weed. The kind of hollow reeds found along certain streams. The kind a man could breathe through while underwater.

Fargo quietly dismounted, letting the reins dangle. He slowly advanced, aware that grass to the north was bending toward him in a beeline. Squatting, he used his left hand to scoop up a handful of the fine dirt.

The grass to the north was bending faster and faster but Fargo ignored it and held his hand over the reed. Carefully, he tilted his palm so the dirt trickled into the opening.

A muffled grunt was the reaction. Tense seconds passed, then the ground exploded upward, erupting like a volcano, spewing earth and dust and the stocky body of a near-naked warrior. The Apache had a revolver in one hand, a long knife in the other. He blinked to clear his vision.

Fargo's Colt leaped out and up. Instead of shooting the warrior, Fargo slammed the Colt's barrel across his forehead hard enough to split stone. The man crumpled like wet paper.

The patter of rushing feet whipped Fargo around. Another Apache was almost on top of him. This one had a revolver on either hip and a rifle slung across his back but he had not resorted to them. Clutched in his right hand was a fine knife with an ivory hilt and an elaborate etching similar to some Fargo had seen south of the border. It was already upraised for a fatal stab. But as swift as the warrior was, he couldn't match the flick of Fargo's thumb and finger. Fargo's Colt boomed twice in rapid succession. As if smashed by an invisible fist, the Apache was flung backward and lay in a disjointed heap.

The blasts drowned out the approach of a third man. Fargo barely heard him in time. Spinning, he had to fling an arm out as another knife descended. Steel rang on steel, the Colt deflecting the blade. The jolt of the impact sent the Colt flying from Fargo's hand. Suddenly he was unarmed, pitted against an enemy who would give no quarter, show no mercy.

Fargo backpedaled as the Apache closed in, the knife weaving a glittering tapestry, slashing high and low, back and forth, up and down. Fargo had no means to retaliate; all he could do was continue to retreat, straight into the grass. Which seemed to be the warrior's intention. For the moment Fargo stepped off the road. The Apache grinned slyly, then bounded to one side and came at Fargo from a new direction.

Fargo twisted, and found out why the warrior had grinned. The grama grass clung to his legs, impeding him. Not much, yet just enough so he was unable to fully evade the next swing. The knife sliced through several of the whangs on his sleeve. Another inch, and it would have bit deep into his wrist.

Grunting, the Apache pressed his assault. He was shorter than Fargo but stouter and superbly muscled. Fargo crouched, making it harder for the warrior to strike a vital organ. He was ready when the blade flashed out again. So did his left hand. He seized the Apache's wrist but to his dismay he couldn't hold on. It felt as if the man's skin were covered with oil. Fargo should have remembered. Apaches often greased their bodies before going on raids, rendering them nearly impossible to grapple with at close quarters.

Fargo dipped to slide a hand into his right boot but the warrior was on him before he could grab the Arkansas toothpick secreted there.

Again the Apache flung his knife arm on high. Again Fargo brought up his arms to ward off the blow. But this time an unforeseen misstep turned the tide of battle in the warrior's favor. As Fargo brought up his arms, he tripped over a cluster of stems. He flailed to stay upright and was on the verge of straightening when the Apache lowered a shoulder and rammed into him with all the power of a bull gone amok.

Fargo crashed onto his back. Frantically, he tried to lever upward but the warrior pounced, landing on his chest. The breath whooshed from his lungs as the Apache straddled him. Glittering dark eyes regarded him with raw delight. Fargo attempted to rise but the man had him pinned.

Realizing it, the Apache grinned and spoke in a thickly guttural tone.

Fargo's knowledge of the Apache tongue was limited. He thought the man said something to the effect, "It gives me great joy to kill you, my enemy." The words were unimportant. The moment's delay it bought Fargo was. He heaved upward, bucking like a bronc, his hips rising a good foot off the ground.

It unbalanced the Apache but did not dislodge him. Clutching the ivory hilt in both brawny hands, the warrior elevated the blade once more.

Fargo was desperate. He couldn't reach his own knife, couldn't throw the man off. He was, in short, as good as dead. He knew it and the Apache knew it. Which explained why the warrior paused again, showing even white teeth, to savor his moment of triumph. Then, shoulders bunching, the man drove the knife at Fargo's throat.

At the very last instant Fargo wrenched his neck aside. He felt the blade scrape him, felt a stinging sensation. The Apache started to pull the knife back to try again. Fargo couldn't let that happen. Luck had been with him once. He couldn't rely on the same miracle twice. So, faster than the eye could follow, Fargo opened wide and clamped his teeth down on the Apache's wrist. He bit with all the strength his jaws could muster, shearing through flesh as if it were soft, boiled venison. The Apache yelped and tried to tear loose but Fargo literally clung on for dear life, grinding his teeth deeper. He tasted the animal fat that had been smeared on the man's body, tasted the salty tang of warm blood.

In great pain, the Apache placed his other hand against Fargo's brow and pushed, seeking to force Fargo to release him. But Fargo's teeth were almost grating on bone. More and more blood gushed. Suddenly the warrior shifted his weight so he could grab the knife with his left hand.

For a span of heartbeats the Apache was off balance. It was the opportunity Fargo needed. Bucking upward again, this time he succeeded in dislodging his adversary. The warrior tumbled to the right as Fargo rolled to the left.

Fargo came up with the Arkansas toothpick in his hand. The Apache had backed off a few feet and was holding the damaged wrist pressed against his midriff. The long knife was now in the warrior's other hand. Fargo glided in low, aiming a cut at the man's legs. Predictably, the Apache countered by lowering his own blade. But Fargo's cut was a feint. Reversing himself, he lanced the toothpick up and in. Although the Apache's catlike reflexes enabled him to avoid being impaled, the toothpick's tapered tip gouged a bloody furrow.

They warily circled, the Apache's eyes blazing with hatred. Fargo dared not take his own eyes off his foe, yet he worried other warriors were rushing to help and might be almost on top of him. He had to end the clash swiftly. Yet how, when he was up against someone as skilled as he was?

Fargo feinted again, then tried for a throat strike. It was no more effective than his first feint. In a flurry he tried all the techniques he had learned, all the thrusts and ruses and counters he had mastered, but each time the Apache thwarted him.

Both of them were breathing heavily from their exertions. The Apache's blade was longer, giving him greater reach, but he couldn't capitalize on the advantage. For Fargo's part, he was debating whether to dash to the road and reclaim the Colt. It puzzled him that the warrior hadn't resorted to a revolver. No sooner did he think it than the Apache did just that.

Fargo had no recourse. He sprang in closer, slicing the toothpick at the warrior's arm. The Apache's knife speared at his face but Fargo ducked under it. A Remington was rising toward him when the Arkansas toothpick connected at last, the slender blade transfixing the warrior's hand.

The Remington fell. For perhaps two seconds the two men looked into each other's eyes, taking silent measure. Then they both lunged to claim the pistol for their own. Fargo was a shade faster. His finger wrapped around the butt and he was rising when the warrior bellowed like a bear and plowed into him, lifting Fargo clean off his feet. The long knife sought his ribs. Fargo grimaced while simultaneously jamming the muzzle against the Apache's torso, thumbing back the hammer, and firing.

At the retort, the warrior stiffened and released Fargo, who staggered back. Straightening, Fargo fired again as the Apache hurtled at him. The slug took the man in the chest and swung him completely around. Teetering, the warrior said something softly to himself, then raised his face to the sky, cried out, and pitched forward, dead.

Fargo backed toward the road. He was sore and bruised and bleeding. Recalling there might be more warriors, he turned, but the grama grass was undisturbed, the road empty save for the two prone forms.

It did not stay empty for long. As Fargo bent to pick up his Colt, the pounding of hooves and loud, familiar rattling fell on his ears. He had been so caught up in saving his hide, he had forgotten about the dust cloud to the east. Toward the knoll rushed a stage, the driver hauling on the reins and shouting for the team to stop.

"Whoa, there! Whoa! Whoa! Whoa!"

Fargo shoved the Remington under his belt and slid the toothpick into its ankle sheath. The dependable Ovaro had ventured several yards into the grass across the road and was patiently waiting. He crossed to it as the stage clattered to a stop shy of the two Apaches. The lead horses whinnied and shied, spooked by the scent of blood, but the driver knew his business and immediately brought them under control.

"Tarnation, mister! What in hell just happened?" asked

the shotgun guard, a short man whose cheek bulged with a wad of chewing tobacco.

"Ain't you got eyes, Larn?" demanded the driver, a grizzled cuss whose homespun clothes were baggy enough to qualify as a tent. A floppy hat adorned a craggy face framed by long hair speckled with gray. "Don't them injuns give you a clue?"

"There's another in the grass," Fargo said, nodding.

The driver half rose to see better. "Lord Almighty! You kilt yourself three Apaches all by your lonesome! That takes some doin'. Either you're the toughest hombre this side of the Pecos, or you're the luckiest critter on two legs." A bushy brow arched as he raked Fargo from head to toe. "The name's Dawson, by the way. Buck Dawson. Best damned driver the Butterfield Overland Stage Company has."

"And not too shy to tell everyone under the sun, either," the shotgun commented dryly.

Fargo gestured. "Give me a hand and you can be on your way."

Buck Dawson wrapped the reins around the brake lever, propped his whip in the boot, then gripped the rail to the driver's box to climb down. "Are you sure you got all them varmints, mister? Apaches are sneaky devils. Might be more of 'em lyin' off in the grass, waitin' to make wolf meat of us and the passengers."

"I doubt there are any others," Fargo responded. Had there been, they would surely have hurried to help their friends.

With remarkable agility for one his age, Buck swung to the ground. "Larn, you keep us covered, you hear? Just in case. We lose any of the folks inside, Clements will have us tarred and feathered." Buck grinned at Fargo, revealing that two of his upper front teeth were gone. "That'd be Charley Clements, our boss. The meanest jasper you'd ever want to meet. Why I keep on workin' for the likes of him I'll never know."

Larn chuckled. "It could be because he's the only human being who will put up with your shenanigans."

Buck Dawson moved to the bodies. "Don't listen to him, mister. He's just sore 'cause all the ladies like me better. He's younger and handsomer, but I've got more spunk. And ladies like their menfolk to have plenty of vinegar and vim."

Faces appeared at the stage window, watching as Fargo crossed the road. A man gruffly demanded, "Why have we stopped, driver? Surely we're not at another relay station so soon?"

"Surely we're not, Mr. Hackman," Buck Dawson responded with a touch of distaste. "Soon as we clear the way, we'll be off. In the meantime, hold your tater." Scrunching up his weathered face as if he had just sucked on a lemon, he whispered to Fargo, "Uppity busybody. Put some folks in a store-boughten suit and they reckon they own the world."

Dawson stooped to grab the wrists of the Apache Fargo had knocked out. Just then the warrior's eyes snapped open and he leaped erect. Dawson screeched like a woman in labor while throwing himself backward.

The Apache made no attempt to reclaim the weapons he had dropped. Pivoting, he streaked into the grass. But as fleet as he was, he couldn't outrun buckshot.

"That one's still alive!" Larn bawled, rising and pressing the scattergun to his shoulder.

"No!" Fargo shouted. He wanted the warrior alive in order to turn him over to the military for questioning, but Fate dictated otherwise.

At a range of twenty feet the Apache took the full brunt of a load of buckshot squarely in the back. He was lifted off his feet and thrown like a child's doll. When he hit, he catapulted end over end until finally coming to rest on his side, his limbs askew, a jagged cavity the size of a watermelon in his chest.

At the selfsame instant, with no forewarning whatsoever, the team bolted. Larn tried to grab hold of the rail on top of the stage for support but the abrupt lurch tumbled him from his perch. With no one in the seat, the stage sped off down the road. Shocked passengers gaped in alarm.

Fargo glimpsed a lovely face topped by hair the color of fire. Rotating, he reached the stallion in three bounds, gripped the apple, and was in the saddle and reining the stallion around before the rear wheel rumbled by. But by then the team was in full stride and he had to spur the pinto to catch up.

"Stop 'em! Stop 'em!" Buck Dawson raved, flapping his arms like an agitated crow taking flight.

Fargo drew abreast of the stage door. He glimpsed the redhead again and the florid face of a bearded man, both shocked by the unsettling turn of events. He lashed the reins to increase speed. In another few seconds he would be alongside the team and could bring them to a stop. But the team, running erratically, caused the stage to swerve sharply. Fargo had to veer off the road to avoid a collision. It slowed him down, costing him precious seconds, and the stage pulled ahead.

"Stop 'em! Stop 'em!" Dawson continued to yell and flap.

Stallion and rider flew like an arrow. Fargo had spent more hours in the saddle than most ten men. He was a superb horseman and he proved it now, racing to overtake the stage, then swinging wide when it swerved toward him as it had before. He could see the woman's white fingers grasping the edge of the window, see the bearded man mouthing a string of oaths.

Another man appeared, a younger man in the type of broad-brimmed hat favored in the rough-and-tumble cow country of central and southern Texas. He had on a faded leather vest and a shirt as well-worn as the hat. Poking his head out, he twisted so he could reach up and latch on to the top rail.

Fargo guessed what the young cowhand was going to attempt and admired the man's grit. The passengers were being bounced around like so many thimbles in a sewing box, so it was hard for the cowhand to keep hold of the rail.

He did, though, slowly pulling himself upward. One slip and he would be dashed to the ground with possibly fatal results.

"Leave it to me!" Fargo hollered.

Either the cowhand couldn't hear over the din or else he thought he could stop the stage sooner on his own because he kept pulling himself higher. He had both hands wrapped around the rail now and over half his body was outside the coach.

Fargo was a few yards behind it and to one side. He dared not ride directly in its wake, causing dust to spew into his face, into his eyes and nose and ears, blinding him and making him cough. A straight stretch materialized. Fargo could gain ground if he wanted, perhaps even pull up next to the team, but he hung back on a hunch the young cowhand was biting off more than he could chew.

Within seconds the hunch was borne out. Clinging to the rail, his whole body swaying violently, the young man eased his legs from the window. All that were left were his boots. But as he hauled himself higher, one of his spurs snagged on the window. He tugged to free it just as the stage gave another jarring lurch. A hand came off the rail and the cowboy swung outward. Gritting his teeth, he clung on, then propelled himself toward the top. He almost made it.

The front wheel hit a hole and the whole stage seemed to bounce in the air. The cowboy's other hand was jarred free and he dropped.

A scream tore from the redhead.

Fargo reined in perilously close to the coach and looped an arm around the man's waist. A yank, a slap of his legs, and they were clear of the rear wheel. The stage pounded on while Fargo slowed to deposit his burden.

The cowboy looked up. "Save them, mister! There are two women inside!"

Fargo needed no encouragement. He let go, then goaded the Ovaro into a gallop. In a way, the passengers were fortunate the team had spooked on the flatland and not up in the mountains where sheer cliffs often bordered the road. All

Fargo needed was another minute or two and he would end their ordeal.

Then another head poked out the window on the other side of the stage. A head adorned with long blond curls. It was a woman, and she was trying to do the same as the cowboy had.

Fargo rode for all he was worth.

2

Skye Fargo was certain the woman would fall before he could reach her. He drew close to the rear of the stage and shouted for her to stay inside. "I'll stop the team!" he added. But as with the cowboy, either she couldn't hear him or she was determined to stop them herself. Whichever the case, she proved smarter than the cowboy in one respect. Instead of clinging to the rail by her hands, she pumped high enough to hook an elbow around it and locked her whole arm tight. In order to do so, though, she had to pull her entire body clear of the window. Her legs swung outward, the blue dress she wore whipping like a sheet in the wind. The hem billowed, affording Fargo a tantalizing glimpse of velvety thighs.

By then Fargo was abreast of the rear wheel. The woman glanced at him and he motioned to let her know he would grab her. Incredibly, she shook her head. Then, in a dazzling display of athletic prowess, she braced her feet against the door and levered upward, flipping up and over the rail onto the roof.

She was safe, Fargo thought. But he was mistaken. The top of the coach was laden with luggage, with trunks and bags and parcels. As the blonde flipped up and over, she hit a large trunk. It unbalanced her and she fell partway back over the side. Suddenly she was in a precarious plight, with the lower half of her body sagging from the rail and no way of bracing her feet for another flip.

Fargo was abreast of her by then but she was too high for

him to reach. "Hang on!" he yelled, and galloped on by. The team still ran flat-out. He considered leaping onto the box and grabbing the reins, but they had been jounced loose from the brake handle. The ribbons were now suspended on either side of the tongue, their ends dangling low beneath the undercarriage.

Spurring the stallion, Fargo swiftly caught up with the lead animals. To grab hold he had to lean half out of the saddle. The horse instinctively pulled away, nearly yanking him off the Ovaro. Thrusting his boots against his stirrups, Fargo hauled backward. The lead horse resisted but gradually began to slow down. When it did, so did the other leader, and that in turn brought the whole team to a sweaty, panting halt.

Wheeling the Ovaro, Fargo rode to the stage. The blonde still clung to the rail. Rising in the saddle, he held out both arms. "Let go. I'll catch you."

Emerald eyes regarded him a moment, then her cherry lips curled and she complied. Fargo slowly eased back down, feeling the warmth of her body against his. He guessed she was in her early to mid-twenties. Her oval cherubic face, darkly tanned, hinted at lots of time spent outdoors. She wasn't one for fashion. Her nails were short and unpainted, her dress rather plain, her shoes unpolished.

"Were you trying to kill yourself?"

The blonde squirmed deliciously as she sat up. "Pshaw! If it weren't for that trunk, I'd have made it up there. Then all I had to do was jump onto one of the last horses, grab hold of the ribbons, and bring the Concord to a stop."

"Is that all?" Fargo said, smirking.

"You think I couldn't? I'm a farm girl, mister. I learned to ride practically before I learned to walk. Anything a man can do, I can do. Usually better. Just ask my six brothers. I could outride them, outshoot them, even outfight them." Pausing, she brazenly placed a hand on his left arm and squeezed his biceps. "Care to wrestle?"

Fargo wondered if maybe all the bouncing around had rattled her brain. "How's that again?"

"You don't know what wrestling is?"

"Of course I do, but—"

"But ladies don't wrestle, is that it? Well, this gal does. You've got more muscles than my brothers and you're a heap bigger than they are, but I'll bet I can pin you quicker than you can bat an eye. What do you say?"

The door opened. A portly man whose cheap suit and dusty bowler branded him a drummer declared in amusement, "Honestly, Miss Pearson. If I'd had any idea Missouri women were so forward, I'd have settled there long ago."

"What's so forward about asking a fella to wrestle, Mr. Tucker?"

Tucker glanced at Fargo, "Do you see what we've had to contend with since leaving St. Louis? I tried to give her my seat behind the boot to spare her from having to sit on the middle bench. And do you know what she said?"

The blonde finished for him. "I said my backside is just as hard as any man's and can sit anywhere a man's can."

Fargo and Tucker both laughed. Fargo moved the Ovaro away from the coach so the passengers could alight. As he was lowering Miss Pearson, the bearded man who had been on the other side filled the doorway and glowered like a bear roused too soon from hibernation.

"What in hell is so humorous? We could have been killed just now, gentlemen, and you act as if we'd taken a carriage ride in Central Park!"

"Oh, please, Mr. Hackman," Tucker said. "What we just went through was nothing. You should do as much traveling as I do. I was on a stage once when a wheel came off while we were going around a curve high in the Rockies. Another time, a driver lost control on a grade and the stage crashed into a stand of trees."

Hackman, indignant, stepped down. He wore a suit and a straw hat. "I really don't care to hear any more of your silly stories. Why is it drummers feel compelled to talk people to death, anyway?" Before Tucker could answer, Hackman turned to Fargo and jabbed him in the leg. "As for you, climb on up and turn the coach around. Hurry it up. We can retrieve the others and be on our way with scant more delay."

Fargo rested his hands on the saddle horn. "There are two things you should know," he said.

"Eh?" Hackman's forehead knit. "What are you talking about?"

"First off, I don't work for Butterfield. The stage sits where it is until the driver gets here." Fargo leaned down so only Hackman, Tucker, and Miss Pearson heard his next comment. "Second thing, if you ever poke me like that again, you son of a bitch, I'll break off your finger and shove it down your damn throat." With that, he dismounted.

Hackman turned apple red.

Tucker started to cackle, then smothered his mirth with a hand.

Miss Pearson nodded. "About time somebody put you in your place, Mr. Hackman. If you don't mind my saying so, you're just about the rudest person I've ever met."

From the door tinkled feminine laughter. "My, my. Aren't we the friendliest bunch you ever did see? I can't tell you how much I look forward to being cooped up in this shoe box with all of you for days on end."

It was the redhead. Despite the heat and the dust, she was radiant. Her hair was neatly brushed, her dress immaculate, her features as beautiful as a sunset. Her lips and nails were lushly red, her figure an hourglass, her bodice twice as ample as the blonde's. Simply put, she was stunning. Ignoring the others, she sashayed toward Fargo and held out her hand, saying, "Melissa Starr, kind sir. Since these louts have neglected to do so, permit me to thank you for saving us."

Fargo accepted it, but rather than shake, he pressed his mouth to her knuckles and lightly nipped them with his teeth.

Melissa Starr didn't bat an eye. "Aren't you the gallant

one?" Grinning impishly at Miss Pearson, she said, "I envy you, Gwendolyn, my dear, being rescued by this handsome stranger."

Gwendolyn folded her arms. "Shucks. I didn't hardly need no rescuing. I can take care of myself."

"You poor, poor child," Melissa said, even though she didn't appear much older than Miss Pearson. "Perhaps one day you'll learn to be comfortable with your womanhood."

"What exactly does that mean?"

"Only that if you ever hope to marry, you shouldn't go around bragging how you can outdo men. A little helplessness goes a long way in winning a man's affection." Melissa saucily fluttered her eyelids at Fargo. "I warrant our knight in buckskins knows exactly what I mean?"

Another man climbed from the stage and came over to introduce himself. "I want to express my gratitude, too. William Frazier the Third, of the Ohio Fraziers." He said it as if it should mean something. Frazier was dressed in the most expensive clothes money could buy and wore several gold rings large enough to gag a chipmunk. A gold watch chain adorning his vest was added evidence of his wealth.

Next, Fargo met Tommy Jones, a boy in his late teens who was painfully shy, and two friendly Italian men whose mangled English was downright amusing. That made a total of nine passengers, about average for an Overland run. Often the company crammed people on the roof, too, to boost revenue. It might sound strange to someone who had never taken a stage, but many travelers preferred to ride on top. They enjoyed a little more room and could stretch out flat when they needed to sleep. The only drawback was being exposed to the elements.

Not that there was much room to spare anywhere. A Concord was eight and a half feet long and five feet wide. There were three seats, or benches. Those at the front and back could brace themselves against the coach but those using the middle seat had to grip leather straps hanging from above. With three people per seat it was cramped, to put it mildly.

Someone once calculated that each passenger was limited to fifteen square inches of space.

Despite the close confines, a Concord was a fine conveyance. The seats were upholstered. Coaches boasted oil lamps and basswood panels. The running gear was made of hickory, elm, ash, or oak. Roll-up leather curtains kept out dust and rain or let in air. Thanks to three-inch oxhide strips ingeniously designed to absorb most of the bouncing and swaying, passengers were spared severe jars and jolts.

Fargo had ridden in stages but only when he had no other choice. The cramped confines weren't for him. He'd rather ride, rather set his own pace, and be lulled to sleep by yipping coyotes than the petty squabbling of tired travelers.

Now, as the passengers stretched their legs and chatted, the cowboy arrived. Thumbs hooked in his belt, a big Smith & Wesson on his left hip, he sauntered up to Fargo and smiled in genuine friendliness. "I saw everybody else pumpin' your hand so I reckon I should do the same. The handle is Burt Raidler. You saved my hash, mister, and I ain't likely to forget. Anytime you need a favor, you just ask."

It was rare to find a Texas cowhand taking a stage. Like Fargo, most punchers preferred to go everywhere on horseback. He made a comment to that effect.

A lopsided grin creased Raidler's mouth. "You've got that right, pardner. If I had my druthers, I'd rather ride a cactus than be cooped up with a passel of chatterbox city folks. But I got into a bit of a scrape and had to leave the Pecos country in a hurry." The grin evaporated. "About rode my poor dun to death. I made it to the next town and sold her for stage fare. Caught the next one passin' through, and here I am."

Fargo didn't ask what sort of scrape Raidler had been involved in. It wouldn't be considered polite. "Where's this stage bound for? California?"

"San Francisco," Raidler confirmed. "But I'm only paid

up as far as Tucson. I figure I can get a job with a local out-fit and earn enough to buy a new horse before too long."

The St. Louis to San Francisco run was one of the longest routes operated by the Butterfield Overland Stage Company. Almost twenty-eight hundred miles, over some of the roughest terrain in all creation. Normally the trip took from twenty to twenty-five days, depending on weather and other factors. Heat, cold, rain, snow, dust—passengers endured them all. Small wonder most people regarded stage travel as an ordeal rather than a luxury.

Fargo spotted the driver and the shotgun messenger off down the road. He turned to the Ovaro to fork leather but a sultry voice stopped him.

"Leaving so soon, handsome? Whatever for? Don't you like our company?" Melissa Starr had the vixenish ways of a woman who was supremely confidant of her beauty and who knew just how to use it to her best advantage. Fragrant perfume sheathed her like a cloud as she gave Fargo the sort of look no man could mistake.

"The company is just fine," Fargo said, hungrily roving his gaze over the swell of her breasts, then lower, to the enticing outline of her thighs. "But I'm headed east, not west."

"Too bad." Melissa adopted a mock pout. "It might be fun to get to know one another a little better."

Over by the rear wheel, Hackman snorted in irritation. "Really, Miss Starr. Must you be so obvious? There is another lady present, you know. And some of us do have more morals than a randy goat."

Fargo stared hard at the bearded malcontent, who glared back a moment, then walked around to the far side of the coach. The man was a sterling example of why Fargo disliked stage travel.

"I don't know what his problem is," Melissa remarked. "He's been grumpy ever since he climbed on the stage in St. Louis. All he cares about is getting to California just as fast as he can." She smiled at Fargo. "Some people just don't know how to relax and enjoy life, do they? But I bet you do."

Fargo regretted not having met her at another time, another place. He had a feeling she would be a regular wildcat under the sheets, the kind of woman he would love to spend a couple of days with. "I do my best."

The drummer, Tucker, had been hovering nearby like a vulture waiting for an animal to die. Doffing his bowler to Melissa, he addressed Fargo. "Say, friend. I couldn't help but overhear. You're heading east? Then you must have a lot of country to cover. How are you fixed for starting fires? In my trunk I have some of the finest matches ever made. A new phosphorus kind. They're called Instantaneous Lighters, and they're guaranteed to work the first time, every time, or your money will be cheerfully refunded."

"Virgil, give your tongue a rest," Melissa said when the drummer paused for breath.

"My dear woman," Tucker responded, "you can't possibly expect me to pass up a potential sale. Selling is my life. It's in my blood." Shouldering her aside, he said to Fargo, "What do you say? A whole box of chemical marvels for only five dollars! Fifty superior matches for so paltry a price! You'll never have to worry about starting a fire again."

Fargo tried to keep a straight face. "What happens if they get wet?"

"Wet?"

"I cross a lot of rivers, a lot of deep streams. And I get caught in the rain all the time. Do these precious matches of yours work if they get wet?"

Virgil Tucker was shrewder than he looked. "Well now, friend, that's a good question. And to be perfectly honest, no, they won't." He brightened. "But you see, that's where the other item I can sell you comes in real handy. I'd like to interest you in a waterproof cloth invented by a gentleman in Philadelphia. Wrap your matches in it and—"

Fargo held up a hand. "I'm not interested."

"But you haven't heard me out. Wait until I extol the virtues of Professor Cavendish's Miracle Cloth! Why, you've never seen the like. It has a thousand and one uses. Besides protecting your matches, it can keep your guns and knives and whatever else you'd like safe from moisture. Have a family heirloom, such as a watch or a ring, that you don't want to rust away? Wrap it in the Miracle Cloth and your worries are over."

"I don't own any heirlooms."

Drummers were a peculiar breed. They roamed the length and breadth of the West, sometimes selling a single product, sometimes a whole line of goods. Whatever the case, they all had a particular trait in common. Not one of them knew how to take no for an answer. Virgil Tucker sidled closer and lowered his voice. "That doesn't matter. You do have that fine pistol, and I see a Henry in your saddle scabbard. So I'll tell you what I'll do." He licked his lips. "Normally, I'd sell the Miracle Cloth for the miserly price of fourteen dollars. But since you just stopped our runaway team and probably saved our lives, I'm willing to chop two dollars off. I'll sell you the matches *and* the cloth for the paltry pittance of seventeen dollars. Now I ask you, is that a bargain, or is that a bargain?"

Fargo couldn't make up his mind whether to shoot him or punch him.

"What's the matter? Still too high? All right. How about if I shave another dollar off, out of the kindness of my heart. Sixteen is all I'm asking. What do you say?"

"Go pester someone else."

"You can't mean that. How many times does a deal like this come along?" Tucker draped a hand on Fargo's shoulder. "My friend, you drive a hard bargain. I knew you were shrewd the moment I laid eyes on you. So I'll slash one more dollar off. Now we're down to fifteen. I'll barely make ten cents profit, but for you, since I really like you, I'm willing to make the sacrifice. How'd that be?"

There was only so much idiocy Fargo would abide. "I

don't want your matches and I don't want your cloth. But there is one thing you can sell me."

"Really?" Tucker beamed. "You name it, it's yours. What do you need?"

"A gag I can shove down your throat."

Tucker recoiled as if he had been slapped, then removed his hand and said sheepishly, "No need to be so testy, friend. I'm only trying to make a living." Acting hurt, he walked off.

Again Fargo turned to the Ovaro. But he had barely lifted his boot when someone called out.

"Hold on there, mister! You ain't leavin', are you? I'd like to bend your ear a minute, if you don't mind."

The driver and the shotgun guard had walked the better part of a mile. Sweat beaded Buck Dawson's brow and he was covered with dust. Larn had gathered up the guns belonging to the slain Apaches, which he carried to the boot.

"About what?" Fargo asked.

Dawson glanced at the passengers, then shuffled off into the grama grass and beckoned. Removing his floppy hat, he wiped his face with a grimy sleeve. "I know I ain't got no right to ask this," he said when Fargo joined him, "but I'd be obliged if you'd do us a big favor." Dawson made sure no one else was within earshot. "I'm a mite worried. There's been talk of that new Apache leader, Chipota, being seen hereabouts. Maybe you've heard of him? He's bragged on how he'll drive every last white from the territory."

"I know all about him." Fargo was going to explain that he had been asked by the colonel at Fort Breckenridge to keep an eye out for Indian sign and leave word at the relay station across the San Simon if he saw any, but the driver had gone on.

"Then you know he's a murderin' devil who's butchered whole families. Women, kids, they're all the same to him. If they're white, he kills 'em."

"Get to the point." Fargo had an idea what Dawson was leading up to. He watched Melissa Starr walk over to Gwen-

32

dolyn Pearson and say something that made the farm girl laugh.

Buck Dawson cleared his throat. "Well, it's like this. I doubt those three bucks you made wolf meat of were by themselves. I figure they're part of a larger band. Chipota's band. I think maybe they were lyin' in wait for some pilgrims to come along and made the mistake of jumpin' you."

"You have it backwards."

Dawson cocked his head. "Are you tellin' me you jumped *them*? Either you're plumb loco, or the bravest cuss since ol' Andy Jackson. Why would anyone want to pull a stunt like that?"

"Would you rather I'd let them attack you?" Fargo rejoined.

"Oh. No. Good point." Dawson saw William Frazier III come toward them, and hesitated. But the wealthy passenger drifted toward the coach instead. "If I'm right, we run a good chance of running into more Apaches. Especially since the next stretch is where they've acted up the most."

With good reason, Fargo mused. From where they stood, the road steadily climbed into the San Cabezas Mountains. To get across the range, the stage had to go through Apache Pass, the highest point on the run, at over five thousand feet. There was a spring near the Pass, a spring the Apaches regarded as theirs and theirs alone. Intruders were invariably driven off.

"So what's all my blabberin' got to do with you? I'll give it to you straight, mister. Larn and me would be awful obliged if you'd see fit to ride with us a spell. Say, past Apache Pass? Maybe even as far as Tucson?"

Fargo had expected as much.

"An extra gun would come in real handy if we ran into trouble," Dawson quickly said when he received no answer. "It's not for my sake, you understand. Or for any of the men. It's for the ladies. That little blonde is as sweet as sugar. And Miss Starr I know real well. She's got a heart of gold. I'd hate for the Apaches to get hold of either of 'em."

So would Fargo. Apaches rarely kept white women as captives. Too weak, the Apaches felt, to withstand the rigors of Apache life. The best Gwen and Melissa could hope for was a swift death. But given Chipota's fondness for torture, they would probably suffer greatly, for many hours on end, before being put out of their misery.

"I'm sorry to impose, askin' to put your hide at risk for a bunch of strangers and all. Hell, I wouldn't even be doing this if we had a few more hombres like Raidler along. He's got sand, that puncher."

"I'll do it," Fargo said softly. Too softly. Dawson didn't seem to hear him.

"But take a gander at the others. Tucker's a drummer, and when it comes to a fight, it's been my experience drummers are about as useful as tits on a tree. Elias Hackman is in business in New York, or some such, so I doubt he'd know his pecker from a pistol. That Jones kid is green as grass. Frazier is hard to judge 'cause some of them rich fellers ain't got no more backbone than a worm. And as for those Italian gents—"

"I'll do it," Fargo repeated.

"You will?"

"Only as far as Ewell's Station. You should be safe enough from there on."

Dawson exhaled in gratified relief. "I'm in your debt, mister. The Apaches will think twice about tangling with us with an outrider along." Clapping Fargo on the back, he walked to the road and held his arms aloft. "I need your attention, folks. Everyone give a listen."

The passengers converged, Elias Hackman standing off by himself. Larn had climbed onto the seat and was examining the rifle he had taken from the dead Apache.

"What has you glowing like a firefly, Buck?" Melissa Starr asked. "I haven't seen you this happy since that weekend you spent at the bawdy house in Nebraska City."

Fargo wouldn't have thought an old-timer like Dawson

could be embarrassed by anything, but the driver sputtered like he had swallowed tacks.

"Now see here, Miss Starr. Just 'cause we've been on a few runs together doesn't give you the right to get personal." Dawson tried to appear angry but failed miserably. "As to why I'm tickled, it's because this feller here—" The driver stopped and faced Fargo. "Land sakes. I forgot to ask who you are."

Fargo told him.

Dawson's lower jaw dropped. Up on the stage, Larn straightened as if he had been prodded with a pin. Virgil Tucker appeared ready to faint.

Gwendolyn Pearson and some of the others noticed. The blonde looked from one to the other in confusion, then asked, "What's gotten into you? You look as if a cougar just ate your prize calf."

Buck Dawson was all teeth—except for the two that were missing. "We don't need to fret about makin' it through now. Not with the Trailsman to help us."

"The who?"

Dawson chortled. "Hellfire! Where've you been livin', girl? In a cave? Why, the Trailsman is just about as famous as Kit Carson and Jedediah Smith combined. Ain't a trail he hasn't traveled, an injun tribe he hasn't fought. With him along, all of you can relax and enjoy the ride."

Fargo knew the driver meant well but he wished Dawson wouldn't lay it on so thick. Truth was, he was just one man. From accounts given by the few survivors of Chipota's raids, the wily Apache had over twenty warriors under him. If the three Fargo had slain were indeed part of Chipota's band, then the passengers would be lucky if they reached Ewell's Station alive.

3

Before the stage had gone another mile, trouble began.

They had left the grama grass and were climbing toward the distant Pass. With the change in elevation came a change in vegetation. Manzanitas sprang up, small trees with glossy red bark. Prickly pear cactus fringed the road. They saw yuccas. Or rather, Skye Fargo did, because none of the others were interested in the countryside. The big stallion easily paced the stage. Fargo roved from one side of the road to the other and from front to back, always on the lookout for sign.

The passengers had rolled up the leather curtains to let air in. Some dozed. Elias Hackman and William Frazier III were reading. Virgil Tucker pitched a product to the two Italians. Melissa and Gwen chatted.

No one acted the least bit worried about Apaches, and Fargo partly blamed Buck Dawson's little speech. They figured they were safe with him along to protect them. So they weren't as alert as they should be. It could prove to be a costly mistake.

The first hint of trouble, though, did not come from Apaches. It came with a grinding thump that lifted the right side of the coach into the air, followed by a sharp crack when the stage thudded back down. The rear gave an abrupt lurch and dipped toward the ground. Inside, one of the women cried out as one of the men swore. Buck Dawson quickly brought the team to a stop, then hopped down to learn the cause.

Fargo already knew. He was behind the stage, on the left edge of the road. On hearing the thump he had swiveled and spied the jagged spine of a partially buried mass of stone jutting four or five inches upward, a stone once completely buried but long since exposed by the steady flow of wheels and hooves.

Ordinarily, it wouldn't pose a problem. Stage wheels were designed to take heavy abuse. Sturdy curved sections known as felloes fitted seamlessly together to form the rim, which was braced by heavy spokes. A thick hub lent extra support, as did an iron band around the outer rim. Normally, wheels were immune to bumps, holes, and rocks.

Usually. Not always. Wheels were known to break on occasion. Since a broken wheel meant delay, and since delays cost a stage company money, worn wheels were regularly replaced. Sometimes, just parts of a wheel had to be repaired; whatever it took to keep the stage line running on time.

Now, Buck Dawson hunkered and vented colorful curses, ending with, "If I ever get my hands on the jackass who's to blame, I'll blow out his lamp!"

Fargo kneed the pinto around for a better look. A section of outer rim had snapped like a dry twig. Three of the spokes were broken. The stage wasn't going anywhere until the wheel was mended or switched.

"Lookee here," Dawson said, pointing at where two of the spokes fitted into separate sockets. It was obvious they had not been aligned properly. "Back in St. Louis I'd noticed a crack in the rim. So they had it fixed by a new kid Overland just hired. A sprout so green, he had clover growin' out of his ears." Dawson smacked the rim in irritation. "Damn me! Why didn't I check his work before leavin'?"

Frank Larn was leaning against a body panel. He spat tobacco juice, then remarked, "We can't fix it on our own, hoss. I reckon one of us has to ride back to the way station on the San Simon and have Harry bring his tools."

"You go," Buck Dawson said.

"Why me? Someone has to guard the passengers."

"Fargo's here," Dawson reminded him. "And I need to catch up on my sleep. The next stretch is the roughest of the whole trip. You wouldn't want me dozin' off as we were going around a curve, would you?"

"You ornery cuss," Larn said. "You've had plenty of rest. The real reason you don't want to go is you're plain lazy. But this time you've outfoxed yourself. I'll gladly do it. Harry's wife makes the tastiest pie this side of the Rockies, and Harry always keeps a full jug in his cupboard."

"Just don't dawdle. With any luck, we can get this fixed and be on our way by nightfall. As it is, we'll be six or eight hours off the pace. Charley Clements will have a conniption."

The driver and the shotgun messenger unhitched one of the lead horses. Larn mounted bareback and trotted off. Most of the passengers had climbed down to watch him depart. Other than Elias Hackman, none were particularly upset. It was a temporary delay, a routine part of traveling by stage.

Hackman fidgeted as if he had ants crawling all over his skin, muttering under his breath the whole while. At last he marched up to Buck Dawson, who had taken a seat on the shaded side of the stage.

"Is this the type of service a customer can expect? The Overland is supposed to be one of the best stage lines in the whole country. Do you expect us to endure inconveniences without complaint? I, for one, intend to write the president of the company and give him a piece of my mind."

Dawson regarded Hackman as he might a bug he wanted to squash. "You do that, mister. Just don't give him too big a piece, 'cause from what I can tell, you ain't got much to spare."

"Now see here!" Hackman balled his fist and took a step.

Dawson rested a hand on the Remington on his hip. "I wouldn't, were I you, pilgrim. When I was hired, the company made it plain they wouldn't take it kindly if I killed a payin' customer. It wouldn't be good for business, they said. But they also told me that if a passenger was ever being a nuisance, I could take whatever steps were needed to make him behave." Dawson paused. "How much fussin' and fumin' can you do without kneecaps?"

Hackman stalked off, muttering again.

Fargo dismounted and tied the Ovaro to the rear boot. He was going to sit by Buck but the musky scent of perfume gave him pause.

"Feel like stretching your legs, handsome?" Melissa had a closed pink parasol resting across her shoulder. "I know I do. We probably won't get another chance like this until we reach Tucson." She offered her elbow.

Fargo took her arm. They strolled toward a cluster of manzanitas, the sun hot on their faces. Melissa opened her parasol and held it between them so they would both benefit. The sensual sway of her hips took Fargo's mind off the heat, to say nothing of her luscious lips, as inviting as ripe strawberries. Fargo felt a stirring in his groin and wished there were somewhere they could go to be alone. "What do you do for a living?" he asked to make small talk.

"You haven't guessed? I tread the boards." Melissa grinned when he gave her a quizzical look. "I'm an actress, Skye. I learned the craft from my mother, bless her soul. Maybe you've heard of her? She was billed as Lovely Lilly, and she played most of the bigger theaters back East until consumption brought her low."

"Can't say as I have."

Melissa shrugged. "No matter. She was a fine, spirited woman, who taught me the two most valuable lessons of my whole life."

Fargo waited for her to say what they were and when she didn't, he prompted, "What might they be?"

"Never take guff off anyone. And anything a man can do, a woman can, too." The redhead thoughtfully twirled her parasol. "That might not sound like much to you, but you're a man. You don't know how hard it is for a woman to make ends meet, to compete with men on their own terms. There aren't as many opportunities for us."

The lament was a common one west of the Mississippi. Fargo had heard it before. But men could hardly be blamed for a state of affairs over which they had little control.

Much of the West was still unsettled; whole regions had not even been explored. Violence was part and parcel of everyday life. Simply staying alive was a daily struggle. So it was no mystery why men outnumbered women ten to one. Good jobs were few, jobs women were willing to take even fewer. Not many of the fairer sex cared to spend twelve hours a day deep in a mine, or busting their backs working a claim, or shooting and skinning buffalo for weeks on end.

Eventually, it would all change. As more and more towns and cities sprang up, as the untamed wilderness gave way to cultivated fields and the plow, more and more women would stream westward to take advantage of the new opportunities.

Melissa reversed the spin of her parasol. "I'm on my way to California to open at the Variety Theater in San Francisco. The owner wrote me to say men there will fall over one another to see a talented performer. He assured me he can sell tickets for as much as sixty-five dollars apiece. And the Variety has over seven hundred seats. Just think! Fifty percent of each evening's take will be mine."

"You'll be rich in no time," Fargo quipped. Talent, though, had little to do with it. In a land where women were as scarce as hen's teeth, men starved for female companionship would pay anything just for the privilege of being near one for a while.

"I recite Shakespeare, read poetry, and sing," Melissa elaborated. "I really can't hold a note very well but no one seems to mind."

Fargo had once attended a performance in the foothills west of Denver where a plump matron had warbled off-key for over an hour while prancing around a small stage dressed in her nightclothes. To call it awful would be charitable. Yet the grizzled prospectors, rowdy drunks, and hardscrabble vagrants who attended had cheered and clapped loud enough to be heard in Mexico.

Melissa leaned toward him, their shoulders and arms brushing. "I've heard that you don't intend to go all the way to Tucson with us. Maybe you should reconsider. It might be worth your while." At that, she impishly winked.

Fargo bent to ask her what she had in mind, intending to run his mouth across her ear. But someone came up behind them.

"Mind if I join you?" Gwen Pearson asked. "I can't stand to sit around listening to Mr. Hackman gripe. I swear, that man can't go five minutes without complaining. Before this trip is done, he might drive me to drink!"

"Feel free to come along," Melissa said sweetly, but Fargo detected a trace of resentment. Apparently Melissa wanted him all to herself.

The farm girl wasn't the only one who hankered to join them. "Wait for me!" Burt Raidler declared, thumbs hooked in his gunbelt as always. "I'd rather spend my time in the company of you fair ladies than with old Buck. He scratches and picks at himself so much, I'm afeared he's got fleas."

Melissa sighed. "Bring everyone, why don't you?"

The four of them sat in what little shade the manzanita afforded. As the sun climbed, so did the temperature. The next few days promised to be scorchers, yet another reason Fargo was eager to head north. Arizona in the summer was an oven.

The women prattled about the latest fashions. Raidler leaned against the tree, pulled his hat brim low, and was soon asleep. That left Fargo to keep an eye out for hostiles. Thankfully, none appeared.

At one point Fargo spotted tendrils of dust to the west, in the vicinity of the Pass. It was unlikely to be Apaches. They seldom made their presence known until it was too late. He guessed it might be someone who had left Tucson that morning, heading east. But after a couple of hours went by and no one came along, he figured he was mistaken.

A third hour passed uneventfully, then a fourth.

Fargo had calculated it would take Frank Larn no more than two hours to reach the way station, another two and a half to return. So he didn't begin to worry until the sun was well on its westward descent. Leaving the ladies to their discussion of the merits of white lace, he walked to the road and gazed eastward. A shadow floated up beside his.

"Frank should've been back by now," Buck Dawson said.

"We'll give him another hour. Then I'll go see what happened."

"And leave us alone?" Dawson clucked like a mother hen worried about her brood. "I'd rather you didn't. It'll be dark by then."

"Apaches rarely attack at night."

"True, but they're not above sneakin' into a camp and makin' off with whatever they can steal. Horses, guns"—the driver nodded at the redhead and the blonde—"womenfolk. With you gone, that'd leave only Raidler and me to protect 'em. Hardly enough."

The man had a point, Fargo reflected. "How are you fixed for water and grub?"

"We have a full water skin in case of emergencies. But the only food is some jerky I brought along for me to munch on. Not enough for a meal for everyone, if that's what you're thinkin'."

Fargo mulled what they should do in case Larn didn't show. There wasn't enough cover nearby to shelter them from the wind, let alone Apache arrows and lances. The passengers would be better off staying in the coach, cramped as it was.

"Maybe Harry wasn't there," Dawson speculated. "The next stage ain't due through for a couple of days. He might've gone huntin' so he'd have fresh meat on hand."

"Maybe," Fargo said. But the station operator wouldn't go far from the station and leave his wife alone.

"Pardon me, gentlemen."

William Frazier III was unruffled by the heat. He had a

polished mahogany cane tucked under his left arm, a hand-kerchief in his right hand. Someone who didn't know better might swear he was out for a pleasant Sunday stroll.

"What do you want, fancy pants?" Dawson asked.

"I don't mean to be a bother, but it has struck me that something is terribly amiss. Mr. Larn should have been here by now, shouldn't he? I was wondering what you plan to do, and if I might be of any help?"

"That's awful decent of you—" Dawson began, then fell silent.

To the east a black dot had appeared, a speck that gradu-ally grew, acquiring form and dimension. Presently all of them could see it was a horse. A riderless horse, lacking a saddle, flying toward them as if a horde of ravenous wolves nipped at its heels.

"I don't like this," the driver said.

Fargo moved to intercept the animal, to prevent it from racing on by, but it had no such inclination. Sixty feet out it slowed. Caked with sweat from mane to tail, its legs un-steady, the exhausted animal walked right up to him with its head hung low. Dry blood matted its back and left side. A wicked cut on its flank and another on its neck showed how close it had come to sharing its rider's fate.

"Dear Lord," William Frazier III declared. "It's the horse Mr. Larn took!"

The others hurried over. Alarm spread. Questions were hurled at Dawson, who stood numb with shock.

"What does this mean?" Elias Hackman's voice rose above the rest. "Where on earth are Larn and the station op-erator?"

Fargo rubbed the animal, which pressed against him. "Larn never made it to the station. There won't be anyone coming to fix the wheel. We're on our own."

Hackman sniffed as if at a foul odor. "Surely you jest? Are you saying that we're stranded? That the Butterfield Overland Stage Company expects us to spend the night out here in the middle of this godforsaken wasteland? Why, this is unpardonable. I must bitterly protest such shabby treatment."

Fargo saw Buck Dawson's face harden but he couldn't reach the driver in time to stop Dawson from spinning and grabbing Elias Hackman by the front of the shirt.

"Don't you get it, you miserable bastard? Frank Larn is *dead!* He was one of my best friends, and the Apaches got him! Now they'll be comin' after us!"

Hackman pried at the driver's fingers. "Unhand me, you lout. And quit trying to scare us. I happen to know all about these craven savages you're so afraid of. I read about them in the newspaper. They'd never attack a party our size." He succeeded in removing Dawson's hand. "I say that either Fargo or you should ride back and obtain the tools we need. If you hurry, we can still get under way by midnight."

Buck Dawson threw back a fist but Fargo gripped his wrist.

"It won't help any."

"No, but it would make me feel a whole lot better!" Disgusted, the driver turned away, his whole body shaking with barely contained wrath.

Melissa Starr pushed past the Italians and young Tommy Jones. "Is Buck right, Skye? Are the Apaches after us now?"

"They could be," Fargo admitted. Especially if it was Chipota's band, and Chipota had any inkling the stage had been disabled. The renegade would never pass up such a tempting target. "Larn might have been made to talk before he died." The colonel at Fort Breckinridge claimed Chipota spoke passable English.

Virgil Tucker doffed his bowler and nervously wrung it. "What do we do, then? Head back to the last station? We could take the team horses, ride double. There's enough to go around."

Burt Raidler pointed out the flaw in the drummer's proposal. "We'd be ridin' right into those Apaches, friend. I don't know about you, but I don't much like the notion."

"Then what do you suggest we do, cowboy?" Hackman

demanded. "Sit here and twiddle our thumbs until help comes? Not exactly the most brilliant suggestion I've ever heard. But then, what else can I expect from a man who herds cows for a living?"

The Texan faced the New Yorker. "What I suggest you do, mister, is to start totin' hardware. 'Cause if you ever insult me like that again, you'd better dig for your blue lightnin' before I do."

Gwen stepped between them. "Please. Now's not the time for petty squabbles. We have a serious situation on our hands. If we're not careful, we'll wind up like poor Mr. Larn."

Everyone quieted. Most stared at Fargo, waiting expectantly. William Frazier III expressed the sentiments they all shared by saying, "We need your guidance. You're the one person here who has had a lot of experience in this regard, unless I'm greatly mistaken. So what do you think is the best course of action?"

Fargo didn't mince words. "Burt was right. We can't go back. And if we stay put, we're no better off. The Apaches will be here by sunup. They'll surround us and pick us off one by one." He nodded at the Dos Cabezas Mountains. "We should keep going. We'll reach Apache Pass in a few hours and can spend the night at Puerto Del Dado Springs—"

Elias Hackman snorted. "You want us to abandon the stage? To abandon all our belongings? And what makes you think we'll be any safer there than we are here?"

His patience strained to the snapping point, Fargo told them about the dust he had seen. "Odds are there's another party already there. They made an early camp. If we hook up with them, we stand a better chance."

"Maybe it's a bunch of freighters," Virgil Tucker said hopefully. "We can ride in their wagons."

"Or maybe it's soldiers," Tommy Jones piped up.

"A patrol!" Tucker exclaimed. "Why didn't I think of that? We'd have an army escort the rest of the way!"

The prospect excited them. But Fargo knew better.

Colonel Davenport had told him the army was cutting back on the number of patrols, a move dictated by the growing shortage of personnel as more and more troopers were sent East in anticipation of the coming clash between the northern and southern states. "I'm down to a skeleton roster now," Davenport had mentioned. "Which is why I can't spare anyone at the moment to check the road east."

"Soldiers!" Gwen Pearson clasped her hands as if giving thanks for Divine Providence. "Then what are we waiting for? Shouldn't we head out while we still have light?"

It took ten minutes to unhitch the team. Fargo and Burt Raidler did most of the work. Buck Dawson hadn't budged since the lead horse returned. Chin against his chest, his eyes closed, he stood as still as a statue.

Elias Hackman, moping his brow, tramped over to Fargo. "Didn't you mention something about springs?"

"Puerto Del Dado. Up in the gorge."

"Maybe it's best we go, then. Even an Apache would wilt in this stifling heat."

Which showed how little Hackman knew. Apaches were trained to run incredibly long distances without tiring. Younger ones tested their endurance by taking a mouthful of water and then jogging four or five miles over the roughest of terrain without swallowing it. Adults could run seventy miles in twenty-four hours with only short stops for rest.

Hackman climbed into the coach and reappeared with a black valise. Melissa Starr started to follow his example but Fargo said loud enough for all of them to hear, "We need to travel light. Just the clothes on our backs."

"I'm not leaving this behind no matter what," Hackman stated, embracing the valise as if it were a lover.

"Is it worth risking your life over?"

The New Yorker clutched it tighter. "You don't understand. If anything happens to this, I might as well dig my own grave and jump in. You see, I'm a stockbroker, and—" He suddenly stopped, as if fearful he had revealed too much.

But Raidler laughed. "Mister, if you're a bronc buster,

I'm the Queen of Sheba. You wouldn't know a hackamore from a hairbrush. I'd wager a year's wages the only thing you've ever peeled is an orange."

"No, no, not that kind of stock," Hackman said. "I deal in securities, in bonds and financial stocks on Wall Street."

"What's that?" the cowboy asked.

"You've never heard of Wall Street?" Hackman was stupefied. "Where the New York Stock Exchange is located? The business center of the entire country? It's where the greatest men in America rub elbows and make decisions that affect the rest of us."

"Rich hombres always have liked to lord it over the rest of us. I reckon they figure all that money makes them special. But all it really does is make them rich."

Fargo placed a hand on Buck Dawson's shoulder. "Are you up to moving on?"

The driver opened his moist eyes, then swallowed. "Sorry. Didn't mean to get all choked up. But Frank and me went back a long ways. He could be a cantankerous cuss, yet he'd give me the shirt off his back if I needed it." Taking a deep breath, Dawson turned. "I heard what you said about the dust. I hope you're right." He saw Virgil Tucker trying to scramble up on the horse Larn had used. "Ever notice how drummers and puny brains go hand in hand? What in blazes is that lunkhead doing?"

Fargo went over. "Pick another animal, Virgil. This one is about done in." Taking the reins, he retrieved the Ovaro and stepped into the stirrups. Melissa and Gwen had already climbed onto one of the horses, the Italians on another, William Frazier III and Tommy Jones on a third. That left two horses and four men. Burt Raidler claimed the next and allowed Buck Dawson to swing up behind him. Which left Hackman and Tucker, who began to argue over who should climb on the last animal first.

Half wishing the horse would kick them both in the head, Fargo asked Raidler and Dawson to collect the guns from the front boot, along with the water bag and the jerky. Then he took the lead, holding to a brisk walk.

The sun was about to relinquish the heavens to the stars. Long shadows spiked outward from the mountains, casting the chaparral in premature twilight. As was often the case at sunset, the wind picked up. A brisk breeze from the northwest brought welcome relief from the heat, but it also brought something else, something only Fargo noticed. His keen nose registered the scent of smoke long before they were to the top. He didn't think much of it. He assumed it was from the campfire belonging to whoever raised the dust earlier. But when he was within an arrow's flight of the crest he detected another scent, and immediately reined up.

It was the acrid tang of burnt flesh.

4

"I don't deem it prudent to split up if there are savages about," Elias Hackman declared much too loudly.

They were off the road, hidden in a gully that paralleled it, the horses being held by Tommy Jones and the two Italian immigrants. Ahead was the notorious Pass. Beyond, the road wound through a deep gorge four miles long, rightfully regarded as the most dangerous stretch in all Arizona. More attacks had taken place along those four miles than in any other area in the territory.

Fargo resisted an impulse to slam the Henry's stock against the stockbroker's temple. "I said to whisper. Or do you *want* the Apaches to know we're here?"

Burt Raidler had a Spencer, and less self-control. The cowboy jammed it against the New Yorker's side. "Leave him to me. If he so much as makes a peep while you're gone, he'll eat his teeth."

Fargo turned to Buck Dawson. "Are you ready?"

The driver nodded. "Ready as I'll ever be. Sneakin' around in the dark with Apaches nearby is a mite harebrained, if you ask me. But I'm game if you are."

"Stay close. When I stop, you stop. Don't speak unless I do."

"Don't fret, mister. I ain't hankerin' to get killed. I owe those vermin for Frank, and I aim to make 'em pay."

Fargo didn't like the sound of that. "No shooting, either, unless I give the word. Savvy?"

"You can count on me."

Fargo hoped so. He scanned the group one last time, then pivoted. Melissa gripped his arm and pulled closer, her breath warm on his ear. "Come back to us, you hear? I'd hate for anything to happen to you, handsome."

Apache Pass lay still and quiet under the pale glow of the stars. Deceptively so. Fargo's instincts warned him the night crawled with life. The two-legged kind. Plucking Dawson's sleeve, he cat-footed to the road and angled to the west. Low hills flanked them. Above the hills towered the high battlements of the gorge, rearing like ramparts on a be-nighted castle. Here the odor of smoke was stronger, as was the smell of burnt flesh. It might easily be mistaken for the scent of roast venison or antelope by someone who didn't know any better.

The Puerto Del Dado Springs were Fargo's destination. That was where travelers would camp. It was the only water close to the road between the San Simon and the San Pedro. It was also where travelers were most vulnerable. Espe-cially along about sunset, after campfires had been made and food put on to cook and tired wayfarers were relaxing after a long, hard day.

Apaches were fierce but never reckless. They always struck when their enemies were off guard. And to an Apache, anyone not an Apache was an enemy, a belief taught to their young from the cradleboard on. Since the dawn of time, Apache legend had it, the way of the warrior had been the Apache way. Or, as Colonel Davenport once put it, "It's the Apaches against the whole world." They had resisted the Spanish, the Mexicans, and now the Americans. They had raided every tribe within a hundred miles, prov-ing their superiority in warfare time and again. The Mari-copas, the Pimas, they all lived in constant fear of Apache depredations.

Off down the gorge a flickering point of light appeared, giving Fargo pause. A single campfire burned. Crouching, he waited for shadows to flit across it but none did. Nudg-ing the driver, he veered across the road and on around a hill, placing each foot down with exquisite care, always avoiding dry patches of brush and loose rocks. His companion was not quite as skilled. Once a twig cracked under Dawson's boot. Another time, a pebble was sent skittering. In each instance Fargo tensed but the sounds apparently went unheard.

Presently a dark mass loomed close to the road. Fargo slanted toward it, every nerve tingling, every sense primed. The squat outline of a building materialized. Until a few months ago it had been an Overland relay station. The famous Chiricahua leader Cochise had personally given permission for it to be built, but treachery by an overeager army lieutenant resulted in the deaths of the station staff. Since the military was unable to guarantee around-the-clock protection, the company decided to abandon it rather than risk more lives.

As silent as a ghost, Fargo glided to the rear wall. Built of stone, the station was a favorite resting place for those taking the Tucson-El Paso Road. The springs were six hundred yards away.

Fargo moved to the corner and peered out. The latest arrivals had pitched camp halfway between the buildings and the springs. He counted four wagons parked in a semicircle. Freighters, out of Tucson. Glowing embers marked the location of other campfires that had almost burned out. Eleven of them. Far too many. He glanced at Dawson. "Whistle if you hear or see anything. I won't be long."

"If you think you're leavin' me here alone, you're loco," the driver whispered. "Those devils will slit my throat before I can holler for help."

Against his better judgment, Fargo let Dawson come. It didn't surprise him the man was so afraid. Even seasoned veterans of Indian campaigns had qualms about fighting Apaches. Comanches, Blackfeet, the Sioux—they were all widely respected as bold fighters. But the Apaches were the most widely feared tribe of all.

Flitting from tree to tree, bush to bush, Fargo came near

enough to see the crackling flames, the burning pieces of wood. The odor of charred flesh was so potent, he pulled his red bandanna up over his mouth and nose. The camp appeared to be empty. Fargo studied it from behind a boulder for a good fifteen minutes. Nothing moved. No horses, no mules, no oxen. No humans. When he straightened and advanced, the driver was glued to his side.

Buck Dawson's eyes were wide with fright. He walked woodenly, as if terrified that Apaches would rise up out of the earth to slay them. Which, considering what had happened to Fargo on the road that day, wasn't as farfetched as it seemed.

Two smoldering piles of wood and ash were near the fire that still burned. Fargo guessed the freighters had made several shortly after they stopped for the night. A typical mistake. They thought that the more light they created, the safer they would be.

Since there were usually two men to a wagon, there had been eight, all told. Fargo found boot and moccasin tracks, mingled in confusion. Evidently the Apaches had snuck in close enough to take the unsuspecting whites alive. There had been a frantic hand-to-hand struggle. And then?

The answer was on the near side of the wagons.

Beside each front and rear wheel glowed coals. Tied to the wheels, heads down, were the mule skinners. Strips of cloth had been stuffed in their mouths. Their hands and feet were largely untouched but their faces and shoulders were blackened almost beyond recognition.

"Oh, God!" Buck Dawson exclaimed, forgetting himself. Doubling over, he retched, shuddering as if it were thirty below.

Fargo couldn't blame him. The Apaches had resorted to a favorite pastime, roasting captives alive. Fires had been built under each freighter. Their hair was gone, their skulls charred mockeries, eyes burned from sockets, noses and ears and cheeks just so much fried meat. Gobs of body fat and liquefied flesh lay underneath each victim. Fargo had beheld a similar sight once before but his gut still churned and he came near to imitating Dawson.

To take his mind off the horrid spectacle, Fargo searched for more sign. The teams had consisted of mules, six to a wagon. Knowing how fond Apaches were of mule meat, Fargo had a fair idea what the band was doing at that very moment. He tried to determine how many warriors there were, but the darkness made the task impossible. He walked over to Buck.

The grizzled driver had risen and was wiping a sleeve across his mouth. "Sorry," he whispered. "Reckon I'm not as tough as I thought. But I've gotten ahold of myself now."

"We'd better head back."

"Do you think the Apaches will return?"

"I know they will." Fargo pointed at the canvas-covered bed of a wagon, which was piled high with merchandise bound for eastern markets. "They had most of their spoils." Probably because night had fallen before they were done with the captives. So they had gone off to feast on the mules.

Dawson sadly shook his head. "How could they, Fargo? I've heard tales that would curdle the blood, but this—" He left the thought unfinished.

"It was a test."

"Of what? How much a person can suffer?"

"Of how brave the freighters were. Apaches respect courage, but they think we're too brave for our own good."

"How's that again?"

Fargo had heard it straight from the horse's mouth, so to speak. An Apache scout at Fort Buchanan had said yes, they prized courage, but they believed a man must be wise as well as brave. Apaches never rushed headlong into dangerous situations as white men were prone to do. The scout had an example. "When white-skins hear a shot, they run to see who fired. When Apaches hear a shot, we hide and spy on whoever did it from a safe distance. You whites are very brave, but it is a foolish bravery."

Now, motioning for Dawson to hush, Fargo hurried toward the deserted station. A sound from a hill to the south had him worried a few Apaches had been left behind to keep an eye on the wagons. Bent low, he zigzagged to make it difficult for an archer or rifleman to pick him off.

Dawson was breathing heavily when they reached the building. He wasn't accustomed to so much running and darting about. "I need to catch my breath."

Fargo entered the station. The door sagged from the top hinge. A table and several chairs had been overturned, a cupboard was on its side. Broken dishes and other belongings of no value to the Apaches had been scattered about. The interior smelled of must and dust and urine. Fargo backed out.

"I heard something," Dawson whispered, jerking a thumb at the hill.

"Let's go."

Fargo didn't waste another second. If Apaches had spotted them, the warriors might trail them to the gully. He must be sure he had shaken any pursuit before he rejoined the others, or all the lives of those on the stage were forfeit.

Rather than head due east, as he should, Fargo bore to the southeast. Dawson realized they were going the wrong way and snatched at his sleeve but Fargo pressed a finger to his lips and gestured for the driver to keep jogging. They swung around a small hill, threaded through trees and among boulders. Crossing a clearing, Fargo dashed to the left and crouched at the base of a slab of rock the size of one of the wagons. Dawson hunkered behind him, panting.

"Cover your mouth," Fargo directed.

It was well he did.

Hardly sixty seconds went by when a pair of shadows detached themselves from the vegetation and cautiously crept forward.

Fargo sensed movement beside him. The barrel of Dawson's rifle poked past his head. Grasping it, Fargo tilted the muzzle up and gave Dawson a stern glance. Then he handed Dawson the Henry and palmed his Arkansas toothpick.

The warriors were halfway across. They halted. One scoured the hard-packed ground, the other kept watch. One held a rifle, the other a bow with an arrow notched to the sinew string. Their faces were shrouded in murk.

Fargo gathered himself as they came nearer. The tracker was lightly running his fingers over the earth, trying to read by touch what his eyes could not discern. A grunt of annoyance brought the second warrior to his side. They conferred in whispers. Apparently, one of them wanted to keep looking and the other to go back, no doubt to report to the rest of the band. The one who desired to go back prevailed. Like ethereal specters, they vanished into the gloom.

Dawson let out a loud breath.

Fargo reclaimed the Henry, but he didn't move until he was convinced the pair were long gone. Backstepping, he hastened around the boulder and sprinted to the northeast. In order for the driver to keep up, he had to go slower than he liked. It couldn't be helped. But it delayed them so that it was another half an hour before they approached the gully's mouth. Fargo's anxiety mounted when no one appeared to greet them.

"Where's the Texan?" Dawson asked. "Wasn't he to stand guard?"

No sooner were the words out of his mouth than someone bawled, "Halt! Who goes there? Identify yourself or I'll shoot!"

Leery of being shot by mistake, Fargo squatted. "Virgil? Is that you?"

"What an idiot," Dawson muttered.

The drummer stepped into the open, a rifle wedged to his shoulder. "Fargo? What took you so long? Where have you been? It's just awful!"

Fargo reached Tucker before the jackass could shout again, clamping a hand over his mouth. Out of the gully bustled Melissa Starr and Gwen Pearson. Both commenced to jabber but Fargo silenced them with a sharp motion. "Stay calm. Tell me what happened."

"The horses are gone," Melissa said.

"And Tommy Jones and those nice fellas with the curly hair are missing," Gwen chimed in.

"We never heard a thing," Melissa took up the account. "Burt went to check on them and found they had disappeared. He's out hunting for them now."

Gwen's blond head bobbed. "He took Mr. Hackman and Mr. Frazier, although Mr. Hackman didn't want to go."

Fargo removed his hand from Tucker's mouth and had to wipe spittle off on his shirt. "How long ago?"

"Not more than twenty minutes," Melissa said.

Gwen agreed. "Do you figure maybe the horses wandered off? That maybe Tommy and those fellas went looking without saying anything to us?"

Fargo credited the three with more intelligence than that. Before he left, he'd impressed on them that under no circumstances should they let any of the team stray. Tommy and the immigrants were to keep the team bunched at the far end of the gully. It should have been easy to do, as narrow as the gully was.

The Ovaro was a whole different matter; it would never drift off on its own.

"Stay with the women," Fargo told Dawson.

"Be careful," Gwen said.

Fargo ran flat out. A few twists and turns, several dozen yards more, and he was there. Neither Raidler nor the two city dwellers were anywhere to be seen. The gully was blanketed in blackness so thick, Fargo would need a torch to read sign. He had to settle for climbing to the rim and prowling in search of dirt clods. Only a few turned up, enough to show the horses had been led out in single-file.

Fargo was torn. Should he go after them? Or should he stay to help safeguard Melissa and Gwen? With six others missing—and the Ovaro—what choice did he really have?

He had to pray Dawson and Tucker could hold their own until he got back.

It was slow going. Frequently, Fargo knelt and groped for tracks. They pointed to the northwest, toward the gorge wall. He didn't come across the cowboy or the other two. In due course the ground began to slope upward, broken by boulders and ravines. Fargo passed through a gap between high boulders, his head bent, so intent on not losing the sign that he almost lost his life. The swish of an object cleaving air was all that saved him. Instinctively, Fargo ducked, and a war club struck the boulder on his right. He brought up the Henry but another swing knocked it from his grip. In a blur, an Apache was on him. The club's stone head flashed at Fargo's face. He threw himself to the rear, back through the gap, scraping an arm but evading the weapon.

The Apache hurtled after him, sweeping the heavy club overhead. Fargo grabbed at his Colt, then thought better of it. Only one warrior had jumped him, a rear guard. A shot would alert the others. As the club swept down, Fargo deliberately dropped flat on his back, tucking his knees to his chest so he could slip his fingers inside his right boot.

The Apache mistook the gambit as panic and sprang. One hand clawed to clutch Fargo's throat as he brought the war club crashing down. But in midair he was met by Fargo's feet and catapulted head over heels. Disoriented, the warrior pushed onto his hands and knees, shaking his head like an angry bull.

Fargo leaped, the toothpick's slim blade glittering dully. He thrust at the warrior's throat but the Apache jerked aside and the steel sank into the man's shoulder instead. The war club hissed upward. It hit Fargo, a glancing blow to the rib cage that rocked him on his heels and seared his torso with torment.

A mountain lion could not have pounced more swiftly than the Apache did. Fargo's left forearm absorbed what would have otherwise been a fatal strike. His whole arm went numb. Scrabbling to the side, he surged upright, only to be met by a downward arc of the club. Twisting, he suffered a bashed hip. But his pelvis didn't shatter, so he could still rotate on the ball of his foot and drive the toothpick into the warrior's chest inches from the sternum.

A low groan escaped the Apache. His arms folded, his legs buckled, and he oozed to the ground like so much melted wax.

Fargo staggered to a boulder and leaned against it. His chest felt as if a rib were busted, his hip throbbed. Gingerly pressing and poking, he satisfied himself that no bones were broken. He yanked the toothpick out, wiped it on the warrior's breechcloth, then retrieved the Henry. At a slower pace he resumed the chase, his hip protesting every step. After a while it grew stiff but he refused to give up. Three lives, possibly more, were in the balance.

The wily Apaches had hugged the base of the wall, where it was darkest. Fargo had to hope they kept heading west because he couldn't see his hand at arm's length, let alone prints or clods. He covered a slow, painful mile, growing more and more uneasy about the women, the driver, and the drummer. Just when he was ready to turn around, an outcry to the southwest drew his attention to a faint gleam of light.

Fargo padded toward it. The final dozen yards he covered on his belly, snaking on his elbows and knees.

From the crown of a basin Fargo gazed down on the Apache camp. A solitary fire blazed in the center. On a makeshift spit roasted the haunch of a mule. The others were tied in a string to the south. To the north were the horses, including his pinto. Over thirty warriors were present. Some hunkered, talking. A few sharpened weapons. Others were rummaging through a pile of blankets taken from the freight wagons, the only spoils on hand.

Fargo was more interested in three figures staked out west of the fire. Tommy Jones and the two Italians were spread-eagled. They had been stripped to the waist, their shoes and socks taken. All three had gags over their mouths.

A warrior near the fire rose and spoke at length. From the description Fargo had been given by Colonel Davenport, it was none other than Chipota himself. The scourge of the territory was a short, stocky man whose barrel chest and extremely wide shoulders hinted at tremendous brute strength. A cruel nature was etched in the cold cast of his features, accented by a sawtooth scar on his left cheek, legacy of a knife fight he was rumored to have had with another Apache. He wore a red shirt and brown pants. Around his head was a red headband. Two pistols adorned his waist, as did a bowie and a dagger. Slung over his shoulder was a Spencer. He also had a lance. The man was a walking arsenal, befitting a warrior who had slain more foes than any living Apache. Which was saying a lot.

Colonel Davenport had told Fargo that Chipota's band was made up of malcontents from various Apache tribes: the Chiricahuas, the Mimbres, the Jicarillas, the Mescaleros, even a few White Mountain and Pinal warriors. Most were young hotheads who would rather wage war than negotiate peace, who would rather die in battle than live under the white man's iron thumb.

Originally, only a handful had followed the renegade. But as his raids grew in boldness and savagery, as his fame spread both north and south of the border, more and more men rallied to his cause.

The army was worried Chipota would trigger a bloodbath the likes of which no one had ever seen. Their ranks stretched thin by a steady transfer of men to the East, commanders like Davenport were hard-pressed to check the seething violence. It threatened to erupt into full-scale war at any time. All that was needed was a final spark—and Chipota was just the man to ignite it.

Fargo trained the Henry on the leader's chest. He was tempted, so very tempted. But it would only bring the rest down on his head, leaving Tommy Jones and the Italians completely at the mercy of their captors. First things first.

Fargo would set them free, then bring an end to Chipota's bloody spree. How to go about it was the big question.

But not the only one. Fargo wondered why the Apache hadn't taken Tucker and the women. Either the warriors never realized other whites were at the opposite end of the gully, or they planned on going back later when everyone was likely to be asleep.

As for Raidler, Hackman, and Frazier, Fargo had no idea where they had gotten to. Blundering around in the dark, probably. Or so lost, they were lying low until sunrise so they could get their bearings.

Fargo saw an Apache cut a strip from the haunch, taste it, and smile. It was a cue for the band to fall on the meat like starved coyotes, ripping with knives and hands and then wolfing whole portions without chewing.

For a while they would be occupied. Fargo slid away from the rim, stood, and crept to the north. Heavy brush provided ample cover. He scanned the sky for the Big Dipper to gauge the time but it was blocked from view by the towering heights. His best guess was eleven o'clock or a little past. How he was going to get the three captives out of the basin, find the missing men, and spirit everyone to safety by daybreak was beyond him.

A commotion drew Fargo to the rim sooner than he planned. Several warriors were jabbing the Italians with lances, just hard enough to draw blood. The poor men strained against the stakes, their muffled cries making the warriors laugh. More Apaches drifted over to see what was going on.

Fargo couldn't lie there and let the immigrants be tortured. He had to act, and quickly. Then a warrior placed the tip of a lance on the chest of Tommy Jones and slowly pressed down. The youth squirmed, which dug the tip in deeper, and whimpered, which provoked more laughter.

Chipota, gnawing on a chunk of mule meat, strolled over along with a dozen others. Fargo sighted down the Henry but couldn't get a clear shot. He waited, hoping fortune would favor him. Suddenly Tommy Jones uttered a stifled shriek. It dawned on Fargo that the Apaches weren't merely toying with the three men; they were going to kill them.

Aiming as best he was able, Fargo stroked the trigger. He cursed when another man took the slug meant for Chipota. At the crack, some of the Apaches flattened. Others scattered. Those nearest the north rim pointed at the gunsmoke the Henry had belched, and yelled. A score of rifles were trained on the crest. A volley thundered, the blast echoing off the high walls. Leaden hornets buzzed thickly in the night.

But Fargo wasn't there. He had slid down the bank and was racing pell-mell to the west. Vaulting a log, he searched for a place to hide. Feral yips lent wings to his feet. The Apaches were flowing up the inner slope of the basin like a horde of rabid wolves. They would rapidly spread out, poking to every shadowed nook and cleft.

A thicket barred Fargo's path. He sped around it, careful to avoid inch-long thorns that could shred an arm or leg to the bone. He glanced back and glimpsed furtive shapes spilling over the rim.

The yipping and howling grew to a crescendo.

Facing straight ahead, Fargo came to the far side of the thicket. He was moving so fast, he didn't see a man coming the other way until they were right on top of one another. They both halted in their tracks.

It was hard to say which one of them was more surprised, Fargo or the Apache returning to camp, his arms laden with firewood. But the Apache reacted first. Dropping the branches, he swooped forward like a bird of prey.

5

As the Chiricahua leaped, Skye Fargo hiked the Henry over-head. The Apache's hands were almost at his throat when the unforeseen occurred. The warrior tripped over the falling firewood and stumbled onto one knee. All Fargo had to do was bring the stock crashing down and the man sprawled senseless at his feet.

To the east the rest of the band was fanning out. In their thirst for vengeance the Apaches made more noise than usual. Yipping and howling, they plowed through the brush in a human wave.

Fargo bolted. He ran to the top of a grassy mound—only to find the other side had crumbled, collapsing in on itself, perhaps during one of Arizona's gullywashers. About to go around, he had an inspiration. But could he carry it out in time? Kneeling, Fargo frantically dug at the loose earth. In less than a minute he had excavated a shallow depression the length of his body. Lying in it, he quickly brushed dirt over his buckskins, covering himself with a thin layer. He had to remove his hat so it wouldn't jut up and give him away. Placing it between his arm and chest, he covered the rest of his body, including his neck and face but not his eyes. Then he lay perfectly still.

It was a desperate gambit. In broad daylight it would never work. The Apaches would spot him in a second. But in the dark, with no moon, in heavy shadow, he might pull it off. In any event, it was too late to change his mind. Light footfalls announced the arrival of grim avengers.

The Apaches had stopped whooping and howling. They were in deadly earnest now, moving like ghosts. Fargo heard a whispered word, then more excited whispers as they surrounded the man he had knocked out. A low groan signified the warrior was coming around. More footsteps drummed, and suddenly a bulky silhouette was perched on top of the mound, directly above him.

Fargo had not covered his eyes so he could see if the Apaches spotted him. He saw the warrior look right and left, but not down. The man spoke over a shoulder and two more breechclout-clad wraiths appeared. One threw back his head and shouted. Fargo need not be fluent in their tongue to know the warrior was letting the rest of the band know their quarry was heading due west. Then the trio bounded off. One stepped on the dirt that covered Fargo's shin, sending a sharp pang up his leg.

Fargo didn't move. Not yet. Furtive rustling and swishing arose on all sides. He waited until the sounds dwindled, until the night was as silent as a tomb. Cautiously, he raised his head high enough to scour the area. No cries rang out. Rising into a crouch, Fargo replaced his hat.

Now he must move faster than ever.

Fargo ran to the thicket, skirting it on the right. Speed was crucial but he was not about to make a blunder that would get him killed. He moved as quietly as the breeze. Which explained how he came upon a warrior without the man being aware of it.

Fargo recognized the Apache he had knocked out. The Chiracahua was shuffling toward the basin, hands pressed to his head. At the last instant the warrior sensed he was not alone and started to turn. Maybe he assumed it was another Apache. Or maybe his head hurt so badly, he simply wasn't thinking straight, because he did not act alarmed. He turned slowly, straight into the descending stock of Fargo's rifle.

Another twenty yards and Fargo reached the slope. He counted on the darkness screening him as he climbed. That, and the fact the Apaches were scouring the landscape in the opposite direction. Tucked low to the ground, he paused on the crown long enough to verify none had remained behind.

For once things worked out just as Fargo wanted. The captives and the animals were unguarded. All he had to do was cut the men and boy loose and they could be on their way. By the time the Apaches realized they had been tricked, he and the others would be long gone.

Running to the spread-eagled figures, Fargo hunkered and drew the Arkansas toothpick. "Don't worry," he whispered to Tommy Jones. "I'll have you free in a moment. How bad are you hurt?"

The youth didn't answer.

Fargo bent over Jones's right arm and applied the toothpick to the rope. "Can you ride? We have to light a shuck."

Again the youth failed to respond. Fargo leaned closer, saying, "I almost forgot about the gag." He reached for it, then saw an inky puddle spreading outward from Jones's neck. The youth had been cut from ear to ear.

Slit just like a fish.

The immigrants had suffered the same fate. Fargo recalled how happy they had been to be in America. They were so friendly, so outgoing. So eager to start new lives. Their dream had been to open a restaurant, to have a business of their very own. To one day bring their sweethearts over from the Old Country and raise families. Instead, their corpses would rot under the hot sun and by next summer all that would remain of their hopes and dreams would be bleached bones.

"Damn."

No one but the Apaches could say why they had done it. Maybe out of spite over having one of their own shot down. Maybe for the hell of it.

Fargo quickly searched the pockets of the three and found a few letters and papers which he crammed into his own. They might contain addresses, someone he could write to. Or he might turn them over to the army and let the government break the bad news to the next of kin.

Suddenly, the Ovaro nickered.

Without delay Fargo raced to the horses and shoved the Henry into the saddle scabbard. Unwrapping the stallion's reins only took an instant. He slashed the tether rope but left the team attached so they would be easier to manage. As he forked leather, several silhouettes reared above the west rim. A harsh cry fell on his ears. He reined the stallion around, tugged on the lead rope, and trotted eastward.

Fortunately for Fargo none of the warriors were armed with rifles. Arrows whizzed, though, as he barreled up the slope, one almost nicking his ear. Drawing the Colt, he twisted and banged off two swift shots, forcing the warriors to drop down while he made good his escape.

More cries of baffled fury rose in bloodthirsty chorus as Fargo veered to the south. He had to reach the gully swiftly, and the swiftest way was to take the road. Going overland would slow him down too much. He hoped that Raidler, Hackman, and Frazier had found their way back. If not, they were on their own until he got the women and the other two to a place of safety. Which begged the question, *where*?

The way station on the San Simon River and Ewell's Station west of the gorge were the closest havens. To the east the country was more open, which reduced the risk of an ambush. But Ewell's Station was closer to Fort Breckinridge, and it went without saying the army must be notified of Chipota's whereabouts right away. So which should it be?

Fargo had not made up his mind by the time he came to the road. As yet no Apaches were on his trail but he didn't slacken his pace. In half a mile he was at the springs, passing the wagons with their grisly trophies. The sight of the campfire, which had burned even lower but was not quite out, brought about a change in plans.

Hurrying to it, Fargo dismounted. Extra firewood had been left nearby. Grabbing two thick limbs, he held them in the flames until the ends caught fire. Then he ran to a wagon and thrust the limb in. He thought the firebrand would go out before the goods ignited but flames spread rapidly. Then it was on to another wagon, where he did the same.

As the old saw went, there was a method to Fargo's madness. It was necessary to delay the Apaches, to divert them, and what better way than to bring them on the run to save their plunder?

Mounting, Fargo rode on. He was elated when at long last he set eyes on the gully. He figured Dawson and the others would rush out to meet him, but no one did. Flinging himself from the saddle, he dashed to the opening mouth. A shout of greeting was on the tip of his tongue but he never voiced it.

The gully, or as much of it as Fargo could scan, was empty. His hand dropped to his Colt and he slowly advanced. He thought that maybe they were hiding beyond the first bend, but they weren't. As incredible as it seemed, now the others had vanished, as well.

Frustrated enough to chew nails, Fargo racked his brain for what to do next. They couldn't have gone far. Yet why had they left at all, when he had specifically told them not to? Had the Apaches caught them? Had Raidler returned and talked them into leaving? Where else *could* they go?

Fargo had to find them, but not until he had hid the team. Climbing back on the Ovaro, he crossed the road and pushed southward. Within ten minutes he came upon a dry wash suitable for his purpose. A small tree at the bank's edge was convenient for tying the rope. Turning, he gripped the saddle horn to swing up but froze when clattering stones and heavy breathing warned him someone approached from the west.

Producing the Colt, Fargo darted to the bank and pressed against it. A darkling shape hove out of the night, running down the middle of the wash. Flowing hair and a rippling garment gave him a clue who it was. Heady perfume was added proof. He lunged, grabbing her around the waist—and had a wildcat on his hands.

"Let go of me, you heathen!"

Melissa Starr raked her nails at Fargo's face. He had to

jerk back to spare his right eye, declaring, "It's me! Skye! Quit struggling!"

"Oh, God!" The redhead collapsed against him, her cheek on his neck. Tears flowed as she clung to his shoulders. "I thought you were one of them! I've been running and running, terrified they would catch me!"

"Calm down," Fargo said, stroking her silken tresses. Guiding Melissa to a flat boulder, he held her soft body close while she wept and sniffled, her warm tears trickling under his buckskin shirt and down his chest. "When you feel up to it, tell me what happened."

The redhead nodded, but five minutes elapsed before she cleared her throat, dabbed at her eyes, and sat up. "I'm all right now. Have you seen any sign of the others? Where did you get to? What took you so long? And where in the world is Burt Raidler?"

"Ladies first," Fargo said.

Melissa smoothed her dress. "There's not much to tell. About half an hour after you left, we heard footsteps. Tucker was scared to death. He thought it must be Apaches. Buck Dawson was sure it had to be the Texan, or you. So he went to the top of the gully and whistled."

Fargo frowned.

"Someone shot him," Melissa said forlornly. "He tumbled back down, his shoulder all bloody. That stupid drummer panicked and ran off. Gwen went after him, to bring him back, I guess. I yelled for her to stop but she wouldn't."

Simple mistakes, Fargo had learned the hard way, often reaped tragic consequences. "How badly hurt was Dawson?"

"He got right up, claiming the slug only grazed him. I asked him to take off his shirt, but just then we spotted two or three people coming toward us. Apaches, Buck said. He took hold of my wrist and we fled to the other end of the gully." Melissa faltered at the memory. "He was worse off than he let on. His whole side was soaked with blood, and he was staggering like he was drunk. He shoved me, Skye. Told me to flee, that he would hold them off while I got away."

"You left him there?"

"What else could I do?" Tears flowed again. "I pleaded and pleaded. Then an Apache came around the bend and Buck yelled for me to run. Shooting broke out. I didn't want to go but I didn't have a gun. I couldn't be of any help." Melissa rested her forehead on his chest. "I think they got him. There were fewer and fewer shots, then whooping like Indians do. I wish I could have saved him."

Fargo draped an arm across her shoulders. Her fingers brushed his cheek, his chin. The fullness of her bosom filled his mind with images better left alone.

"What do we do now?" she wanted to know.

"Damned if I know," Fargo responded, and meant it. The passengers were scattered all over creation and might well be dead or in Chipota's clutches, for all he knew. Hunting for them in the dark was a surefire invitation for more trouble than he could handle. Twice now he had gotten the better of the Apaches. To chance a third clash would be foolhardy.

"We can't desert them," Melissa said. "Frankly, I don't give a hoot about Hackman. But what about Raidler? And sweet little Gwen?"

"I'll take you to the San Simon relay station and come back for them."

"Who are you kidding? By the time you get back, it will be too late." Melissa raised her head. They were nose to nose, mouth to mouth, so close he could kiss her by simply pursing his lips. "No, I won't be responsible for their deaths. We'll look for them together, now."

The actress had no notion what she was asking. "The gorge is crawling with Apaches. I saw at least thirty, and there must be plenty more."

"You're not even going to try?" Melissa said in reproach, then she pointed and declared, "Goodness! What's on fire?"

From that distance the burning wagons resembled bonfires. Vague forms were visible, moving back and forth. So Fargo's ruse had worked. Chipota and the main part of his band would be busy for a while saving the other wagons. Fargo explained what he had done.

"Aren't you the clever one?" A gleam that had nothing to do with the far-off flames came into her eyes. "Intelligent as well as handsome. You'll make some lucky gal a fine catch one day."

Fargo's skin prickled as if from a heat rash. "You stay with the horses. I'll go to the gully."

"I'm not letting you out of my sight ever again." Melissa threw her arms around him to emphasize her point, and in so doing, her mouth touched his.

To hell with it, Fargo thought, and kissed her. He meant it to be a quick, light kiss, but she uttered a tiny hungry groan and tried to inhale his tongue. Her breasts strained against him as if anxious for release. Unconsciously, his hand drifted to her thighs and they parted to receive him.

Fargo would love nothing better than to savor the redhead's sensual charms, but it was hardly the right time or place. How just like a woman! They always accused men of being as randy as roosters, but the truth was that females were every bit as lustful and had a peculiar knack for picking the most ridiculous moments to give their desire free rein. Reluctantly, he drew back and stood. "Later," he said.

"I'll take that as a promise," Melissa huskily teased.

"Mind riding double?"

"Not at all. But why can't I ride one of the other horses?"

Fargo had his reasons. First and foremost, the Ovaro was the only mount he could completely depend on. The others weren't accustomed to being ridden. They might whinny or do something else that would attract Apaches. Also, he didn't know how much experience Melissa had on horseback. In the dark she might blunder into a ravine, or her mount might act up and she would be unable control it. Rather than say as much, he answered, "It's best this way."

The gully seemed the logical place to start. That was where Raidler and Gwen would return to, if they were alive.

Fargo kept the stallion to a walk, stopping often to rise in the stirrups and look and listen. He didn't know how long the Apaches would be occupied at the wagons. But it wouldn't do to let his guard down.

Melissa Starr didn't help much in that regard. Her breasts and belly were flush against his back, her warmth kindling his own. Her arms, looped around his waist, slid lower and lower the farther they went, so that when they neared the road, they were at his hips, her hands dangling within a finger's length of his groin. No man with blood in his veins could help but imagine how nice it would be to feel their caress.

Then, when Fargo shifted in the saddle to gaze into the gorge, her fingers briefly made contact. The pressure set him to tingling. Hunger raged in his chest, a hunger that had nothing to do with food. Yet he was glad when Melissa straightened and her hands moved.

Shortly, from fifty feet out, Fargo surveyed the gully one more time.

"Why did you stop?" Melissa whispered. "Gwen and the rest might be in there waiting for us."

"Apaches might be waiting, too."

"I didn't think of that. Take your sweet time."

Fargo nudged the pinto. He promptly reined up when a moan fluttered from a cluster of nearby manzanitas. It was repeated a minute later. The Colt cocked, Fargo headed for the shrublike trees. Feeble movement brought him to a prone shape. A floppy hat lying beside it identified who it was.

"Buck!" Melissa was off the pinto in a heartbeat and kneeling by the old-timer. "He's bad off. Help me, please."

They rolled the driver over. Dawson was out to the world. In addition to a gunshot wound below his collarbone, he had sustained a nasty knife cut on an arm and what appeared to be a lance wound in his leg. Judging by how wet his shirt was, he had lost a lot of blood but his pulse was steady and strong.

Fargo slid his arms underneath Dawson to lift him.

"Wait. Are you sure it's safe to move him?"

"Would you rather the Apaches do it?" The driver was heavier than Fargo counted on, but he carried Dawson to the stallion with no problem and placed him, stomach down, over the saddle. He gave the reins to Melissa. "Keep an eye on him."

Hastening to the gully, Fargo inspected it from end to end. Neither Gwen nor anyone else had come back.

"So what now?" the redhead asked when he emerged.

Fargo's response was to lead the pinto down the road.

"Where are we off to now? Are you just going to leave the stage horses where they are for the Indians to find?"

"You're a regular bundle of questions. Ever think of working for a newspaper?"

Grinning, Melissa wrapped her arms around him and snuggled against his left side as if she were cold. "I don't mean to be a bother. It's just that I'm scared, and when I'm scared, I can't stop my tongue from wagging."

There were worse faults, and Fargo said so. "As for being afraid, show me someone who brags they never are and I'll show you a liar."

"You never act scared."

"I learned early in life that if you let fear get the better of you, you might as well dig your own grave. Fear makes you freeze at the wrong moment. The Sioux like to say that fear is a man's only true enemy." Fargo could tell the talk was relaxing her so he continued. "I don't give it a second thought anymore. I just shut it from my mind and do what needs to be done. It's easy once you learn how."

"You're mistaken. I could practice shutting fear from my mind for a thousand years and I'd never be as brave as you are."

Fargo looked at her. "You're an actress, aren't you? Act brave and you will be."

"Is it that simple, I wonder?" Melissa rested her cheek on his shoulder. "I'll have to take your word for it. Were I the best actress in the world, I'd still scream my lungs out if Apaches rushed us."

71

As Fargo recollected, the road curved about half a mile from the Pass. South of the curve grew a stand of oaks. Not a large stand, possibly two acres at the most, yet sizeable enough to provide the cover they needed.

The wind was rustling the leaves when they arrived. It was well past midnight, and Fargo was tired enough to sleep for a week. His hip had grown worse. His ribs objected whenever he raised his arms above his shoulders. He was starved enough to eat an elk raw and thirsty enough to drain the San Simon in a single gulp.

Fargo ushered them deep into the heart of the oaks. In a small glade he halted and carefully lowered Buck Dawson. The driver never stirred. While Melissa examined him, Fargo stripped the saddle and blanket off the Ovaro. He spread out his bedroll, propped the saddle at one end, then opened a saddlebag and took out a handful of pemmican which he offered to the redhead.

"What is this?" Melissa asked, sniffing suspiciously.

"You'll like it better if I don't tell you."

"As famished as I am, I'd eat raw skunk."

Fargo smiled. "It's called pemmican. Indians make it by pounding buffalo meat into a powder, then mixing it with fat and dried berries. Or cherries, in this case. I traded a Cheyenne for some a while back and haven't used it all up yet." He treated himself to a bite. The tasty morsel set his mouth to watering and his stomach to growling.

Melissa nibbled at hers, chewed slowly, then giggled and took a bite big enough to choke a grizzly. "It's delicious. I hope you have five or ten pounds of the stuff. How about some coffee to wash it down?"

"We can't build a fire."

"I understand," Melissa rested a hand on Dawson. "What about poor Buck? Shouldn't we do what we can for him?"

The slug had gone clear through the driver's body, sparing arteries and veins. The knife wound was shallow, the lance wound deep but not fatal. Fargo cleaned all three as best he could without water. While Melissa bandaged them with strips cut from the hem of her dress, he asked, "Any idea what happened to the water skin?"

"Elias Hackman had it last I saw. It disappeared when he did. My guess is he left it somewhere in the gully."

"I'll look for it in the morning." Fargo indicated the bedroll. "You're welcome to stretch out if you like. I'll keep watch awhile, then turn in." He needed to get some sleep or he would be worthless come morning. Exhaustion dulled the senses, slowed the reflexes. To tangle with Apaches he must be razor sharp.

"You're not going anywhere until daylight? It'll just be you and I, here alone?"

"And Dawson."

"Oh. Of course. And Buck."

Fargo indulged in another bite of pemmican. He'd learned his lesson. To try and find the missing passengers at night was like trying to find the proverbial needle in a haystack. There was too much ground to cover, too little light to spot tracks.

Melissa walked to the blankets and stretched out on her back. Sighing contentedly, she patted a spot next to her. "Why don't you make yourself comfortable? I noticed how stiff you are. A massage might do you some good."

Her ploy was as transparent as glass. But Fargo went anyway. The Ovaro would nicker if the wind brought the scent of approaching warriors. He and Melissa were safe enough, temporarily. Sitting beside her, he shoved the last of the pemmican into his mouth and leaned back.

"Do I strike you as crazy?" Melissa unexpectedly asked.

"No. Why?"

"Because there's something I want to do. Something insane, given where we are and the danger we're in. No one in their right mind would ever do it."

"Do what?" Fargo inquired, although he already knew.

"Let me show you." Melissa reached up, grabbed his shirt, and pulled him down on top of her, molding her hot mouth to his.

6

Melissa Starr's lips were exquisitely soft, exquisitely stimulating. Rippling against Skye Fargo's, her mouth inhaled him. Her tongue sought his and whirled in an erotic silken dance. It was a simple fact that some women could kiss better than others, that some kisses were as lifeless as a lump of coal and some were volcanic with passion. Melissa Starr had a quality about her that lent her kisses crackling sexual energy. Fargo could not get enough of them.

Melissa's body rose to meet his as Fargo lay against her. The lush fullness of her bosom held intoxicating promise. It heaved when Fargo placed a hand on her flat stomach. Her knees parted as he roamed his palm lower to the junction of her thighs, a throaty moan escaping her. Greedily, her hands were everywhere, roving over his broad shoulders, his well-muscled back, his tight buttocks. She desired him as much as he desired her, and their pent-up lust threatened to explode with the raw fury of a thunderclap.

Fargo would have liked nothing better than to tear off her clothes and pound into her in unbridled abandon, but a tiny voice at the back of his mind warned him to exercise caution. He mustn't lose himself in his carnal cravings. Part of him must stay aloof, must listen to the night's sounds and test the night air. He must never for a second forget Apaches were abroad, or he would pay for his carelessness with his life.

The sexual fire that flamed in Fargo's veins made him as hard as iron. When they broke apart to catch their breath,

Melissa was panting. She cooed while he kissed her cheeks, her ears. She purred as he sucked on her earlobes, as he tongued her satiny throat. Her fingers entwined in his hair, brushing his hat off, then explored his chest, his hips.

Fargo ground his pole against her nether mound and Melissa responded by thrusting up into him. While his mouth was busy, he pried at the buttons on her bodice, loosening enough of them so the dress parted. Moving her underthings aside, he lowered his mouth to her enormous globes. They were as ripe as melons, their tips as hard as tacks. His lips found a nipple, causing Melissa to quiver in the grip of raw ecstasy. He kneaded it delicately and she groaned. He kneaded it roughly and she clawed at his shoulders as if seeking to rip his shirt from his body.

"Ohhhhh, I want you!"

The feeling was mutual. Fargo dallied at her mounds, giving both nipples their due. He licked her snowy slopes, working around them, then up and down, increasing the heat they gave off and causing her to squirm in boiling anticipation.

"You're good, handsome. You're sooooo good."

Fargo had more practice than most, but he didn't tell her that. He cupped her right breast, kneading it with his strong fingers. Melissa threw back her head, her eyes hooded, her mouth parted in a delectable oval. Her eyelids fluttered when he cupped the other breast and gently squeezed both.

"Harder, big man! Harder! I don't mind it rough!"

If that was the case, Fargo was happy to accommodate her. He clamped his fingers tight. Melissa had to cram a hand in her mouth to stifle a scream of purest delight. Closing his own mouth on her right nipple, he pulled on it, stretching her breast as he might an elastic band, inciting her even further. Her fingernails sank into his upper back, digging deep, sparking pain and pleasure in equal degrees.

For the longest while Fargo dallied at her breasts, stoking her as a blacksmith stoked a forge. He didn't undress her, as he would have liked. It wouldn't be wise, he felt, for either of them to shed their clothes or footwear. But he did unhitch his gunbelt and set it aside, within easy reach.

Melissa mistook that as a sign he was ready to plunge into her. She tore at his pants, undoing them and pushing them down over his hips. Brazenly, her right hand drifted to his organ and her fingers grasped it.

"Ohhhh! You're so big! I had no idea!"

She was a bald-faced liar. Fargo had caught her staring at his crotch several times, like a matron in a meat market assessing the size and worth of a slab of prime beef. She'd had a fair idea of what she was in for, and it had fueled her hunger, not dampened it.

Women had perfected being coy to a fine art. When it came to what went on under the bedsheets, they liked to pretend they were as innocent as angels. To be fair, it didn't apply to all of them. And, the truth be known, while many men traipsed around imitating bull elk in rut, as many males as females were shyer about making love than they were about belching in public. Some folks went so far as to only make love in the dark. They would never undress in front of their lovers, never so much as kiss in front of others. They were the ones Fargo could never quite understand. To him, lovemaking was as natural as breathing. What was there to be shy about?

Now, Fargo felt a tingle shoot up his spine as Melissa began to stroke his member. She ran her fingers up and down, around and around, then cupped him and kneaded him as he had kneaded her. It was all he could do not to explode.

"Are you ready, handsome?"

No, Fargo wasn't. Easing her legs apart, he sank to his knees between them. She guessed what was coming and let go of him. He hiked her dress to her waist, bent, and adjusted her undergarments so her womanhood was exposed. She gasped when he blew on her downy hairs. Her gasp became a strangled cry as his tongue flicked out.

"Ahhhhhhh!"

Fargo licked again, relishing the taste. Melissa was delicious, sweeter than the sweetest fruit, more sugary than a fresh-baked pie. He plunged his tongue into her tunnel and she arched her back, her fingers hooked in his hair.

"Yes! Yes! Keep it up!"

Fargo indulged himself, arousing her to whole new heights of rapture. Melissa was so hot, so wet. Her body responded to his slightest touch, her thighs opening and closing in abandon, her breasts swelling even more. He found her core, and flicked it as he had her nipples. Her reaction was predictable. She bucked like a bronco, her thighs gripping his head like a vise.

Fargo slid his hand over her pillowy backside, along her outer thighs, then up to her giant globes. He glimpsed her face, her expression one of total bliss. Then he rose on his knees and gazed down at her marvelous charms.

Some men liked to praise the wonders of Nature, others were fond of paintings and sculptures, so-called works of art. But in Fargo's opinion nothing could compare to the incredible beauty of a woman making love. In the throes of physical joy, women were prettier than a glorious sunset, more lovely than any statue. Give him a living, breathing woman over a dead painting of one, any day.

Such were Fargo's thoughts as he aligned his pulsing manhood and rubbed it along her opening. She tugged, eager for him to shove it in, but he took his time, inserting his rigid sword inch by gradual inch until he was buried to the hilt.

"Oh! Oh! Oh!"

Melissa grasped him close, her face pressed to his chest, her whole body as still as the eye of a storm. But like a storm, she simmered and roiled with forces she could never control, forces she unleashed when Fargo gripped her by the shoulders, slowly drew his hips back, then slammed into her like a battering ram.

In a steady rhythm, Fargo pounded into Melissa again and again and again. She met his thrusts with thrusts of her own, matching him so they pumped in unison. Their urgency rose with the rising power of their thrusts, their bodies smacking against one another, his mouth and her mouth fused. They breathed as one, moved as one. For all intents and purposes, they *were* one.

Melissa reached the pinnacle of release first. She suddenly stiffened and moaned wildly while her hips churned violently. She came in sobs, repeatedly, and just as she started to slump against him, Fargo's own explosion rocked him upward. He drove into her in a frenzy until he, too, was spent. Together, they sank to the ground and lay in exhausted embrace.

The whole time, part of Fargo's mind had been alert for alien sounds, for the stealthy tread of moccasin-clad feet, for any movement where there should be none. Now he let himself relax. The Ovaro was dozing and so should he. He needed rest, needed it so much he was asleep within seconds and slept soundly until the warbling of a bird snapped him awake.

Hours had elapsed. A faint glow to the east was the harbinger of a new day. Dawn was not far off. Rising, Fargo buckled his pants and strapped on the Colt. Melissa was still asleep, her clothes disheveled, her red mane framing her head like tongues of fire. He gently pulled her dress down, then covered her with a blanket.

A noise brought Fargo around in a whirl but it was only Buck Dawson. The driver had stirred, and his mouth was opening and closing. Fargo walked over just as the man's eyes opened. Hazy with pain, Dawson looked around as if confused by where he was and how he had gotten there.

"The Apaches, remember?" Fargo said, hunkering.

"Trailsman?" Dawson blinked, then tried to sit up. Wincing, he stared at the bandages on his chest, arm, and leg. "They almost did me in, didn't they? I was tryin' to save Miss Starr. I recollect emptyin' my six-shooter, then runnin' until I dropped. How is it you found me and those red devils didn't?"

"Plain dumb luck."

"But Miss Starr!" Dawson propped himself on his elbows. "We have to do something! They were after her."

Fargo pointed at the actress. "She's safe, Buck. I'm leaving to track down the others. Keep her here until I get back."

Dawson sank down and mustered a grin. "Don't fret on that score. I feel weak as a kitten. I'm not going anywhere, and I won't let her go wanderin', either."

Fargo patted the man's shoulder and started to rise.

"Wait. Is it Chipota? Do you know?"

"I saw him with my own eyes."

"Damnation. I wish we could get word to the army. A company of troopers would put an end to that bastard once and for all." Dawson gripped Fargo's leg. "You have to find the others. Please. For me. I'm responsible for them. I've never lost a passenger yet and I don't aim to start now."

"I'll do what I can." In the condition the driver was in, Fargo didn't deem it wise to tell him about the three who had been slain.

After quietly saddling the stallion, Fargo took the pemmican from his saddlebags and gave it to Dawson. "Make sure your pistol is loaded. And keep your eyes skinned."

"Same goes for you, pardner."

The air was brisk but not cold, invigorating Fargo as he made off through the oaks. A squirrel up early chattered at him for intruding on its domain. A small owl took wing, a mouse clenched in its beak.

Morning mist shrouded the gorge. Dew cloaked the grass. Both would burn off with the rising of the sun. Fargo rode at a brisk walk, scrutinizing the stony heights for telltale glimmers or motion. From those rocky crags the Apaches could see for miles.

The sun rimmed the world when Fargo came within sight of the gully. Hauling the Henry from the scabbard, he levered a round into the chamber. This time he didn't dismount. Riding in, he looked for the water skin but found something else.

Virgil Tucker had lost his bowler and his clothes were a mess. His shirt hung out, his pants were ripped, his shoes were scuffed. He was seated against a boulder, snoring loudly. In his lap was a revolver.

Leaning down, Fargo poked Tucker with the Henry. He had to do it three times before the man snorted and sputtered and sat up.

"What? Who?" Terror set in. Fumbling with the Remington, Tucker began to push erect. Then he saw who it was, and sagged. "Oh! It's only you! God, you scared the living daylights out of me."

"Where's Gwen?"

The drummer stiffly unfurled. "Miss Pearson? How would I know? We were attacked last night. In all the confusion I was separated from the others. I have no idea where any of them are."

"You ran out on them when they needed you most," Fargo amended. "She went after you. How is it you wound up back here and she didn't?"

Tucker was ashamed and it showed. "I didn't mean to desert them. Honest. But I've never been so scared in my life." He wagged the pistol. "I never even fired a shot. I just ran and ran and ran. In circles, it turned out. I never saw Miss Pearson. I heard her call my name a few times but I couldn't bring myself to stop. I'm sorry. Truly sorry."

Fargo believed him. "Right now we have more important things to worry about. The water skin is supposed to be here somewhere. Find it for me."

While the drummer hastened off to comply, Fargo pondered. One down, four to go. By now Chipota's band was up and about. If the Apaches had caught Raidler, Hackman, and Frazier the night before, they would spend the day torturing them. If the Apaches had Gwen, she would be spared torture but she might well wish they killed her instead.

The mist was fading fast. To take advantage of it, Fargo had to hurry. He went around the bend to get the drummer.

Tucker, lo and behold, was walking toward him with the water skin.

"I did it! Here it is!"

"Climb up," Fargo said, holding out a hand.

In a quarter of an hour they were at the dry wash. The team was where Fargo had left them. He had Tucker switch to one of them, then told the drummer how to reach the stand of oaks. "Don't leave it until I show up or hell freezes over." When Tucker smirked, Fargo said gruffly, "I mean it. I'm sick and tired of everyone wandering off on me. Do it again and you're on your own."

"I'd rather stay with you, if you don't mind."

"Go."

"I won't be a bother. Honest."

"You already are." Fargo reined the pinto around and waited for Tucker to leave but the drummer didn't move. "What the hell are you waiting for?"

Tucker's lower lip trembled as he gazed out over the inhospitable countryside. "I'm afraid, damn it. I don't want to be alone."

"You won't be once you get to the stand. Now get moving or I'll shoot you myself." Fargo gestured angrily. Shoulders slumped, Virgil Tucker slunk off. He glanced back often in mute appeal but Fargo wasn't about to change his mind. The man would be more of a hindrance than a help.

When the drummer was finally out of sight, Fargo set to work in earnest. He returned to the gully yet again. He had to. To track down Gwen and the missing men he had to start where they did.

In the bright light of the new day tracks stood out as clear as crystal. Fargo found where Virgil Tucker had sped into the darkness. And where Gwen Pearson had gone after him. Her prints were smaller, shallower. She had chased him for over forty yards when Tucker veered to the northwest. Hampered by darkness, Gwen didn't realize he had changed direction. She kept going northward. By the length of her stride it was evident she had been running at her top speed.

Another forty yards, and Gwen's stride changed. She'd slowed down. Soon her tracks were meandering in uneven circles. Fargo guessed that she knew she had lost the drummer. Probably her bearings, as well. Finally she had hiked due east, which in a way was a blessing. She was going away from Chipota's band, not toward it.

Fargo clucked to the stallion. He had high hopes of catching up to her before another hour went by. That is, if she'd had the presence of mind to stop for the night. Once she was safely at the oaks, he would go after Burt Raidler. By the end of the day they would all be reunited and he could lead them to the way station on the San Simon. Their nightmare would be over.

What were those?

A new set of tracks had appeared. They came out from behind a boulder and paralleled Gwen Pearson's. Drawing rein, Fargo slid down and hunched over to inspect them. At first glance they resembled the prints of a mountain lion. They were approximately the same size as those of an adult cougar's, although an exceptionally large one. They had the same general shape, the same general placement of the pads. But certain differences, traits only a seasoned tracker would notice, filled Fargo with dread for Gwen's safety. For one thing, the four pads on the front of each foot were spaced slightly further apart than they would be on a mountain lion. For another, the ridges on the rear pads were not quite as sharply defined. And the tracks were deeper than they should be if a cougar were to blame.

Fargo jumped onto the Ovaro and broke into a trot. Those were the prints of a big cat, sure enough, but a *jaguar's*. It was shadowing Gwen, as it would deer or antelope, and when it was hungry enough, it would close in.

Jaguars weren't common in Arizona, but neither were they all that rare. The Indians claimed that at one time they were as numerous as cougars. In the Bosque Redondo country they were still especially plentiful. Elsewhere, it depended on the availability of game.

Fargo would rather tangle with a dozen mountain lions than a single jaguar. Jaguars were larger, heavier, meaner, less predictable. And unlike most cougars, they weren't afraid of humans. This one was a huge male. From the way it was stalking Gwen, Fargo suspected it had preyed on humans before.

A line of cottonwoods announced the presence of a stream. The farm girl's tracks led into them. Handprints showed where she had knelt to drink. Then she had sat awhile, resting. Unknown to her, the jaguar had been watching from the undergrowth. When she moved on, so did the big cat. It had sniffed at the spot where she sat, then fell into step in her wake, matching her pace.

Gwen had gone south. Perhaps she reasoned the stream would bring her near the road, but it curved to the east later on. She had paused and paced, debating whether to follow it or to strike off across country. Nine out of ten people would stick with the water. But country-bred women had more grit than most. Gwendolyn had continued southward. She must have a hunch that sooner or later she would hit the road, and she was right.

Provided she lived that long. The jaguar had narrowed the distance between them.

Fargo had no reason to think Gwen even knew it was there. The lengths of her stride grew shorter and shorter, showing how tired she was. He marveled that she never halted to catch some sleep, yet it was just as well she didn't. The jaguar would seize the opportunity to seize her.

Then both sets of tracks changed their pattern. The jaguar had stopped. So had Gwen, scuff marks revealing she had turned. Either she saw or heard the cat roar. She ran, and the jaguar fell into a lazy lope. She was at its mercy and the predator seemed to know it. It was in no rush to finish her off.

Fargo raised his eyes from the prints, certain he would soon find Gwendolyn's ravaged body. If so, he would kill the jaguar. Once one developed a taste for human flesh, it became a habit. Laziness was also a factor. Animals disliked hard toil as much as people. And compared to wary deer and fleet-footed antelope, humans were ridiculously easy for the big cats to kill.

Spurring the stallion into a gallop, Fargo scanned the rugged terrain. Gwen might be lying behind any of the large boulders ahead, her body ripped to pieces. He shut the image from his mind. Then, faintly, a voice wavered. So faint, Fargo wasn't sure he had heard it until it was repeated. Slowing, he cocked his head.

"Skye! Here I am! Here!"

Movement at the top of an isolated oak on an otherwise arid slope galvanized Fargo into a gallop. Gwen clung to the uppermost limb, a branch so thin it was a miracle it supported her weight. She waved and laughed for joy, her perch swaying precariously.

"Thank God you've come! I thought I was a goner!"

In a spray of dust Fargo reined up. The jaguar's tracks ringed the base of the tree but the cat itself did not appear to be anywhere around. Vaulting off, he hollered, "Do you want me to come get you?"

"No need! I'm not helpless!" Gwen slid to the next lower branch and from there clambered down with an agility Fargo admired. He saw that she had torn the lower half of her dress off. From the knees down, her legs were bare. Fine legs they were, too. Not as full or shapely as Melissa's but enticing enough to turn the head of any man.

Fargo stood back as she flipped onto the bottom limb, twisted, and alighted beside him as lightly as the beast that had stalked her. She was scraped, scratched, and bruised, her face smudged, her hair a worse mess than Melissa's, but she was alive. "You had me worried," he admitted, and was nearly bowled over when she threw herself into his arms and hugged him tight enough to crack his ribs.

"You weren't the only one," Gwen said softly. "I don't know how much longer I could have clung on up there."

"Where's the jaguar?"

Gwen pulled back and gasped. "How did you—?" She glanced at the ground. "Oh, the tracks. It was here a few minutes ago, then it ran off. I think it heard you coming." Shuddering, she bent her ankle so he could see a bloody slash. "I lost count of how many times it tried to reach me."

Fargo brushed his fingers over a series of deep claw marks on the trunk. Jaguars were good climbers. But their weight restricted them to lower, thicker branches. It had been clever of Gwen to climb so high. He spied part of her dress lying on the other side of the tree, the fabric rent to ribbons.

Gwen noticed and wearily smiled. "The jaguar did that when I flapped it in his face." She brushed at a stray bang. "The pesky critter kept climbing higher and higher. I tried to break a branch to hit it, but couldn't. So with my teeth and my nails, I ripped my dress and shook the piece at him when he climbed too close for comfort."

"You didn't sleep a wink all night, did you?"

"No. And if I don't get some soon, I'll pass out." Gwen stifled a yawn. Her eyes were bloodshot, her features haggard.

Fargo would rather take her to Melissa but an hour's delay wouldn't do any harm. "You can take a nap if you want." Clasping her hand, he moved toward a shelf above the oak. "Not a long one, mind you. I'll stand lookout for the jaguar and the Apaches."

"How are the others?"

Briefly, Fargo related everything that had taken place. She grew immensely sad on hearing about Tommy Jones, Joseph, and Michael.

"I'm beginning to think going to visit my aunt in California is the dumbest idea I've ever had. I'd have been better off writing her a letter."

Chuckling, Fargo avoided a small rock outcropping. He was almost to the shelf when two things happened simultaneously. Gravel under his feet gave way, clattering like so many marbles and pitching him off balance. And on the rim of the shelf a great feline head appeared, its slanted eyes aglow with bestial ferocity.

"Skye!" Gwendolyn screamed.

Fargo tried to right himself and bring the Henry into play but the cat was lightning quick. Snarling viciously, it sprang.

7

Skye Fargo had only raised the Henry halfway but it saved his life. When the big cat slammed into him with its forepaws slashing, the rifle was struck instead of him. The Henry was torn from his grasp as he was flung backward. Stumbling, Fargo recovered and hurled himself to the right to evade another flurry. He hit on his shoulder and rolled down the slope, the jaguar just a step or two behind him, rumbling growls loud in his ears.

Fargo had let go of Gwen as he fell. He was glad the cat ignored her, and he hoped she had the presence of mind to get away while she could.

Then there was no time for thinking. Fargo came to a stop in a sliding rain of dirt and stones. He pushed onto his knees just as the jaguar reached him. It never slowed, never hesitated. Steely muscles rippling, it pounced. Fargo barely got his arms up and the beast was on him. Claws sliced his left arm, his side. He was bowled over and slid further, the cat astride him and trying to rip open his throat with its great fangs.

Fargo was a goner. He could no more slay a jaguar with his bare hands than he could outrun an antelope. Frantically, he clawed for his Colt but one of the cat's legs had it pinned against his side. Nor could he lift his leg to get at the Arkansas toothpick. He stared up into the cat's bristling face, at its gleaming teeth and long whiskers and blazing eyes. He felt its warm breath, tinged with the fetid odor of flesh and blood from its last meal. He was gazing into the face of death, and he knew it.

Poised for the kill, the jaguar paused.

Fargo had always expected to meet a violent end. With the life he led, it was only natural to think a bullet or arrow would bring him low. Or maybe a grizzly would take him unawares. Or he would be caught in a buffalo stampede with nowhere to take shelter. But he had never thought one of the big cats would be responsible. Certainly not a jaguar.

A person could never predict how their life would turn out. Fate was too fond of springing surprises.

Then, unaccountably, the jaguar jerked and snapped its head around. It uttered a coughing roar.

Fargo couldn't understand why until he saw a rock strike it on the side.

"Get away from him! Scat, damn you!" Gwendolyn Pearson had a stone in each hand and was barreling toward the riled carnivore as if it were a house pet that needed to be disciplined. "Go! Leave us be!"

"Run!" Fargo shouted, but she paid him no mind. The cat had momentarily forgotten about him and glared at her, its lips curled, its tail twitching. Fargo still couldn't reach the Colt, but out of the corner of an eye he spied a large rock. As the jaguar turned back to him, he smashed the rock against the side of its head with all his strength. At the same moment, Gwen threw a stone that thudded against its ribs.

The jaguar leaped straight up into the air, a good five feet. It wasn't seriously hurt but the pain had rattled it. By twisting its entire body, the jaguar was able to land so that it faced both of them.

Gwen had picked up another rock. "Go eat something else!"

Fargo saw the cat crouch to spring. It was so close, he could reach out and touch it. He started to go for his pistol but realized that even if he put two or three slugs into it as it charged, there was no guarantee he could stop it from reaching her. So, as the jaguar's rear legs uncoiled, Fargo did the only thing he could think of to save Gwen—he seized its tail.

The incensed jaguar spun, a front paw flashing, but it couldn't quite reach Fargo's hand. It lunged, just as another stone pelted it on the head. In baffled outrage the predator glanced from Fargo to Gwen and back again. It was confused. Prey rarely gave the big cats such a hard time.

"Don't come any closer!" Fargo yelled while making a bid for the revolver with his left hand.

Another stone hit the jaguar, on the tip of the nose this time. Frenzied, it dug its claws into the ground and tore loose from Fargo. The next moment, in a fluid spurt of speed, it bounded off toward a cluster of boulders, moving so fast it was out of sight before Fargo could snap off a shot.

"We did it!" Gwen exclaimed. "We drove it off!"

Fargo stood and dashed to the Henry. They owed their lives to a fluke of feline behavior, nothing more, and he wouldn't put it past the cat to come after them again once it had calmed down. "We're getting out of here," he announced.

The Ovaro was still by the oak. Fargo took Gwen by the hand and hastened lower. "Were you trying to get yourself killed?" he demanded. "Chucking stones at a cat that size?"

Gwen could be sarcastic when she wanted. "I'm sorry. I guess I should have let it rip you to shreds. Oh. And you're welcome for saving your hide."

Fargo stopped. There was no denying he owed her his life. If she'd done as he told her, the jaguar would be feasting on his flesh right that minute. "It's not that I'm not grateful," he clarified. "I'd just hate to have anything happen to you."

"Aren't you the sweet one," Gwen playfully teased. Rising on her toes, she kissed him on the chin, close to his mouth. "I'll take that as an apology."

Grinning, Fargo steered her to the stallion. It stared at the clustered boulders, ears erect. Wishing he could hear what it did, Fargo mounted, then lowered his arm for Gwen to hang on to so he could pull her up. "Are all Missouri girls as brave as you?"

"I can't speak for all of them," Gwen said while straddling the pinto's broad back, "but my folks taught me never to take any guff off anyone or anything. My pa may have been a dirt-poor farmer but he had more gumption than most ten men. And my ma was always at his elbow, through thick and thin." She placed her hands on Fargo's hips. "I miss them both, terribly. The Good Lord called them to their reward much too soon."

"They've both passed on?"

"Pa died about a year ago. An accident. He was clearing trees for new acreage to plow, and one of the trees fell on him. Broke his neck." Gwen coughed. "As for my ma, she just wasted away after pa died. She wouldn't take a bite, wouldn't hardly ever drink, wouldn't do anything but lie there with tears in her eyes. Without him, she said, life wasn't worth living anymore."

"You couldn't force her to eat?"

Gwen's tone became bitter. "Ever try to force-feed someone? It ain't easy. My sisters and brothers and I tried, but we couldn't get much down her. Believe me, Skye. When a person makes up their mind to die, there ain't a whole lot you can do except watch them slowly fade away."

"I'm sorry."

The farm girl shrugged. "That's the way the hog bladder bounces. I lost my grandparents when I was seven and always thought it was the worst thing that ever happened to me. Then my folks up and died. Makes you wonder. Why does the Good Lord let us suffer like that?"

"I'm no parson, Gwen."

She fell silent, and Fargo rode on under the blazing sun.

Ranging wide of a steep-walled ravine, he came upon a broad canyon. Specks circling high in the sky drew his interest, especially when they circled lower and lower and finally merged with the ground ahead.

"Are those what I think they are?" Gwen asked.

"Buzzards," Fargo confirmed.

"Haven't seen any in a long while. There used to be a lot in the woods around our farm, but my brothers used them for target practice."

Eleven of the ungainly carrion eaters had gathered and were tearing at something that lay in dry brush. Fargo slanted to the right. He took it for granted they had found an old cougar kill, or maybe one of the jaguar's. A gust of wind proved him wrong. Loose papers fluttered across the ground, causing the stallion to shy as if at a sidewinder.

"What the dickens?" Gwen said. "Where'd they come from?"

Fargo reined up and swung off. He snagged one of the papers on the fly. At the top of the sheet, in big, bold, fancy letters, were the words "New York Stock Exchange." Below the heading were lists, a lot of names and numbers in separate columns, which he couldn't make any sense of.

"What is it?"

Fargo handed the paper to her and retrieved another. This one was a letter from the law firm of Klempner, Johnson, and Foster. It was addressed to a Brandon J. Leonard in San Francisco and had to do with money Leonard had invested.

"The New York Stock Exchange?" Gwen said. "Say, didn't that grump, Elias Hackman, say he worked there, or some such? That he's a stockbroker, whatever that is?"

Fargo nodded. He'd met a man in Hackman's line of work once. The broker had been as talkative as a drummer, going on and on about how much money there was to be made in stocks and securities. Fargo hadn't paid much attention. He had as much interest in stock and bonds as he had in chemistry.

Another paper rustled by. Fargo was bending to snatch it when he saw the black valise a dozen yards away, on its side. Gwen must have spotted it at the same instant.

"Look! Isn't that Mr. Hackman's?"

She hopped down. Together they walked over, gathering papers as they went. The valise was wide open, nearly empty, the contents scattered close by. Most had to do with stocks and quotes and other financial information as foreign to Fargo as a foreign language. He shoved everything inside, closed the black bag, and rose. The buzzards were engrossed in their grisly feast. "Hold this," he said, shoving the valise at Gwen.

"My word! You don't think—?"

It was hard to say. So many vultures had converged, Fargo couldn't see what they were eating. He slowly approached them, waving his arms and hollering to scare them off. A few took wing immediately. Some hissed and flapped before relinquishing their prize. The last couple merely walked off a few yards and tilted their bald heads to keep an eye on him.

Fargo's stomach roiled. "You shouldn't look," he called out.

Elias Hackman had been dead at least twelve hours. His clothes had been ripped to tatters, his body well on its way to being the same. Something, a coyote possibly, had gotten to it before the buzzards and gnawed his throat to ribbons. Hackman's eyes were gone, a delicacy by scavenger standards. So were his lips, most of his nose, and one ear. Fingers were missing. His stomach had been bit open and coils of intestine yanked out.

"What are you doing?" Gwen asked. "How can you stand to be that close? I'm about to be sick!"

Fargo had seen worse. One time he came upon an entire village of Mandans laid low by smallpox. Men, women, and children lay in droves, rotting where they had fallen. Like most Indians, the Mandans had no immunity to diseases brought in by whites. The tribe had practically been wiped out.

Now, although bile rose in his throat, Fargo squatted to examine the corpse. The scavengers had done so much damage, determining the cause of death would be a challenge. Or so he thought until he noticed a small, neat hole in Hackman's chest. Picking up a stick, Fargo scraped aside what was left of the stockbroker's jacket and shirt. The hole told him a lot. His face clouded and he threw the stick at the two nearby buzzards. One lifted slowly into the sky but the other was unruffled.

"What are you doing, Skye?" Gwen repeated.

Girding himself, Fargo went through the New Yorker's pockets. There was a wallet, a couple of keys, a few coins. And a pocket watch. Not as fine a watch as William Frazier III owned, but fine enough that no self-respecting Apache would pass it up. Apaches delighted in geegaws, in showy trinkets they could take back to their women. Backing off, Fargo rotated.

"What do you have there?"

Fargo showed Gwen the items, then put the watch and the coins in the valise. He checked the wallet before dropping it in. It contained papers Hackman had judged important, including a letter of introduction to Brandon J. Leonard from Stanley Klempner. There was a miniature of a rather plain woman in a pretty bonnet, maybe Hackman's wife, maybe a relative. No money, though, which Fargo found odd.

"Poor man," Gwen commented. "I didn't think much of him, but I wouldn't wish this on my worst enemy." She motioned at the body. Buzzards were alighting to resume their interrupted meal. "Being butchered by Apaches is an awful way to die."

Fargo didn't tell her about the hole he had discovered. When they were back in the saddle, he rode to where the valise had been lying. Hackman's prints were plain enough. Fargo backtracked, reading them as easily as most men would read a book. Elias Hackman had staggered into the canyon from the other end, heel marks showing where his feet had dragged and he had lurched from side to side. Evidently, he had been shot elsewhere. How the man had lasted so long, Fargo didn't know.

Two other sets of footprints muddied the mystery. One set had been made by a man wearing shoes, the other by someone wearing high-heeled boots. The kind favored by cowpunchers.

"Beats me what you're looking at," Gwen commented. "All I see are scratches and scrapes."

"Tracking is like everything else. It takes practice."

"What have you found? Do you think the Apaches got Burt and Mr. Frazier, too?"

"Not that I can tell."

"Then where the blue blazes did they get to?"

At the canyon's entrance the two sets of tracks went in different directions. The cowboy had gone to the southeast, the other footprints bore to the southwest.

"Which way now?" Gwen inquired.

Fargo had another decision to make. William Frazier III was heading toward the gorge, and trouble. Burt Raidler was making for the San Simon. Fargo was inclined to go after the former but he had Gwen to think of. Clucking to the pinto, he reined to the southeast.

"Lordy, I am tired," the farm girl said. She leaned against him, her arms sliding around his waist, her cheek on a shoulder blade. "I don't think I can keep my eyes open another five minutes."

"Doze if you want to. I won't let you fall."

"Thank you, kind sir." Gwen giggled. "My ma would have a fit if she were still alive and saw me acting so shameless. Where we come from, when a gal and a man ride double, it means they've taken a shine to each other."

"I won't tell anyone if you don't."

Gwen didn't say anything. Presently, when Fargo glanced over his shoulder, she was sound asleep. For the next hour he was careful to avoid jostling her more than necessary by fighting shy of steep slopes and talus. Their winding course brought them within half a mile of the road, by his reckoning, when he entered an arroyo. The peal of the stallion's horseshoes on stone was like the ring of a hammer on nails.

Fargo rounded a bend. Gwen's left arm started to slip so he gently grasped her wrist. When he looked up, light gleamed on a spine of earth fifty yards further. It might be the glint of sunlight off quartz. Or off metal. When the light moved so did Fargo. Grasping Gwen tightly, he dived head-first from the saddle—just as a rifle boomed. He tried to shift and grab her to cushion the fall but the drop was too short.

The jolt of hitting the ground awakened her. Crying out, Gwen sat bolt upright, only to be pushed flat by Fargo.

"Stay down or you'll get your pretty head shot off!"

As if to stress his point, two more shots blistered the arroyo, each kicking up dirt within a few feet of where they lay. Thanks to some yuccas, the rifleman couldn't see them clearly. Nor could Fargo see the rifleman.

"Who is it? Apaches?" Gwen asked.

"I don't know yet."

"Who else could it be?"

That, Fargo aimed to find out. Flourishing the Colt, he gave it to her. "In case our friend out there 'gets past me." Like an oversized lizard he crawled to the left. "I'll give a yell when it's safe." Another shot cracked, the slug kicking up dust a foot from his head.

Fargo pulled his hat low and crawled in among slabs of stone almost as tall as he was. A toad hopped out of his path. Ants half the size of his thumb marched by. Past the slabs grew a belt of thorny brush and he worked his way deep into it. Every now and then a barb would poke or gouge him.

Wisps of gunsmoke pegged the position of the shooter. Fargo slid from the brush to the base of an embankment. He was rising when the rattle of a pebble warned him the rifleman had moved. Snaking to the top, he slunk up over the rim and lay flat. He was in the open now, exposed for anyone to see. But as Fargo had suspected, no shots shattered the dry air. He glued his eyes on the end of the embankment, waiting with the patience of the jaguar that had stalked Gwen Pearson.

Into sight crept Burt Raidler. The Spencer was wedged to his shoulder and the hammer was all the way back. He looked right, he looked left, he looked straight ahead, but he didn't think to look up. Sliding one boot forward at a time, he concentrated on the brush. His drawn features betrayed fatigue, and dust covered him like a second skin.

Fargo shifted so he faced the edge, then rose onto the balls of his feet. He let Raidler get directly under him, and leaped. Too late, he realized the sun was at his back. A simple mistake, but one that could cost his life.

Raidler saw Fargo's shadow and spun, elevating the Spencer. For an instant the Texan appeared shocked. The Spencer went off almost in Fargo's ear as he slammed into the cowboy, spilling them both into the dirt. Burt Raidler was last to rise and paid for it with a clout to the skull that dropped him like a poled ox.

Fargo took the cowboy's rifle and six-gun. He searched each of Raidler's pockets but didn't find what he was looking for. Backing off, he called Gwen's name. She came on the run, her shock when she saw who it was as great as Raidler's had been on seeing Fargo.

"Why, it's Burt! What in the world is going on? Why did he shoot at us?"

"Ask him when he comes around."

A groan hinted that wouldn't be long. The cowboy sluggishly sat up, holding his head in his hands, and complained, "Damn, Fargo. I feel like I've been stomped by a mule. You had no call to wallop me like that."

Gwen spoke before Fargo could. "You have no room to talk. Why did you try to kill us?"

Raidler peered up from under his hat brim. "Are you loco, girl? If I'd known it was you, do you think I'd have taken those potshots? The sun was in my eyes. I mistook you for Apaches, is all."

Fargo glanced at the sun, noting its position in relation to where the Texan had been when he fired. It was possible Raidler was telling the truth. It was also possible Raidler had gotten rid of the gun that killed Elias Hackman or hid it with whatever had been stolen, and planned to go back for it later, after Chipota's band drifted elsewhere.

The cowboy jabbed a finger at him. "The sun wasn't in your eyes, hombre. So what's your excuse?"

Fargo watched Raidler closely, gauging his reaction when he said, "Elias Hackman is dead."

"I know. Those mangy Apaches! He was as mean as a stuck snake, and I'll admit I didn't care too hard if they made worm food of him. But he had a right to go on breathin', same as the rest of us."

"The Apaches didn't kill him," Fargo said.

"What?"

"How's that?" Gwen Pearson echoed. "If they didn't do it, who did? That jaguar we tussled with?"

Raidler looked all around. "There's a jaguar in these parts? Where? Those sneaky critters make me as nervous as a long-tailed dog in a room full of rockin' chairs."

Fargo continued to study the cowhand. "It wasn't the jaguar, either. Hackman was killed by a white man. By someone from the stage."

Both were stunned. They started talking at the same time. Then they stopped, and Gwen motioned for Raidler to speak but he shook his head and said, "After you, ma'am. I've got the feelin' I don't know half of what's going on and I'd sure like to learn."

Gwen was a prime example of why Missouri was known as the "Show Me" state. "You never mentioned any of this earlier. What proof do you have Apaches aren't to blame?"

97

"Hackman was shot with a derringer—" Fargo began.

Gwen interrupted. "What's that matter? Apaches use all kinds of guns, just like we do."

Fargo had to concede her point—as far as it went. Apaches were as fond of revolvers and rifles as they were of their traditional weapons. The lance, the bow, the war club, all were relied on in warfare and the hunt. To combat the white man on equal terms, Apaches also armed themselves with Colts, Spencers, and Sharps. But there were some guns they routinely shunned. Shotguns, for instance, which were only effective at short range. Pepperboxes, which had the same failing and often misfired. And derringers, which Apaches—and many frontiersmen—considered beneath contempt, fit only for gamblers and dandies.

"I just don't understand how you can blame one of us," Gwen had gone on.

"I saw the wound," Fargo revealed. "Whoever shot Hackman was so close the derringer left powder burns. It had to be someone he knew. Someone he'd let walk right up to him."

Gwen wasn't convinced. "It could just as well have been an Indian. I've heard people say Apaches can sneak right up on you and slit your throat in broad daylight."

"Apaches wouldn't pass up the chance to torture him. Or to take his watch."

She still refused to accept the idea. "What motive would any of us have? Tell me that."

"The answer was in there." Fargo nodded at the valise. "It was something someone wanted so much, they were willing to kill for it."

Burt Raidler digested the revelations thoughtfully. "And you reckon I'm the one? Is that it?"

"You were there. I saw your tracks."

"Oh, hell. I spotted some buzzards and went for a look-see. Hackman was already dead. I saw his bag and a bunch of papers but I didn't touch any of 'em. They mean nothin' to me."

Fargo would like to believe the cowboy. He would like to believe someone else was to blame. And that the sun really had been in the Texan's eyes. "I want to take your word for it," he admitted, "but until I make up my mind, I'll hold on to your hardware."

Raidler was upset. "Now hold on, hoss. It's one thing to knock me on the noggin. It's another to take a man's means of protectin' himself. I'd be obliged if you'd hand 'em over."

"I can't."

The Texan slowly stood. "Maybe I didn't make myself plain. No one takes my guns. *No one. Ever.* Either give 'em to me or shoot me, 'cause that's the only way you'll keep me from takin' 'em."

"Excuse me?" Gwen said.

"Not now," Fargo told her.

"Hush, little lady," Raidler said. "This is between the Trailsman and me." He edged forward. "What will it be? Are you the kind of polecat who can gun down an innocent man in cold blood?"

Gwen suddenly stepped between them. "This is really important!"

Fargo hadn't taken his eyes off the Texan. He had no desire to hurt Raidler, but he couldn't hand over either firearm until he was convinced it was safe. "What is?" he testily demanded.

"Those two Indians are stealing your pinto."

8

They were Apaches, mounted on mules. One had hold of the Ovaro's reins and was angrily tugging while the other warrior slapped the stallion on the flank again and again. It did no good. The pinto balked, moving slower than a snail.

Skye Fargo could guess why the pair had gone after his mount. The Apaches intended to strand them afoot, then return with more warriors. He couldn't allow that. Snapping the Henry to his shoulder, he sighted on the warrior who held the reins. The Apache looked back and suddenly swung on the far side of his mule, hanging by an elbow and an ankle. An old Comanche trick. But the trick had worked in Fargo's favor in that the Apache had to let go of the reins to perform it.

The second warrior was still slapping the Ovaro. He glanced at his companion, saw what the other man had done, and twisted. When he spied Fargo, he swept up his rifle, a Sharps. He should have done as his friend did.

Fargo smoothly stroked the Henry's trigger. The recoil pushed the stock into him, while forty yards distant the second Apache sprouted a new nostril. Flipped backward, the man tumbled. The mule stopped cold.

The first warrior had goaded his mount into running off. Part of his face jutted from under the mule's belly, but Fargo didn't fire. To bring down the man he must bring down the mule. And unlike some frontiersmen, he was loath to kill anything unless it was absolutely necessary. He disliked hunters who shot more game than they needed. Anyone who killed animals for the hell of it deserved to be shot themselves. He wasn't like Gwen's brothers, who picked off turkey buzzards for target practice.

Part of the reason had to do with the time Fargo had spent among the Sioux. They were mighty hunters, but they never slew to excess and they always used every part of whatever they killed. Buffalo alone provided dozens of everyday items, everything from mittens to soap.

Another reason had to do with a lesson Fargo's widespread travels had taught him. Hardly a day went by that he didn't witness one animal kill another. It might be a grizzly eating fish, a pack of wolves culling deer, a bird of prey swooping down on a rabbit or prairie dog, a snake swallowing a frog, or a bird devouring a worm. The daily parade of death made Fargo realize how precious life was. No creature, from the smallest to the largest, deserved to be senselessly slaughtered.

Now, Fargo lowered the Henry rather than shoot the mule. Inserting two fingers into his mouth, he whistled shrilly. Obediently, the stallion trotted toward him. As for the mule belonging to the dead man, it was more interested in grazing than in running off. Fargo smiled. The extra mount would come in handy.

Then a hard object gouged into the base of Fargo's spine and he heard the click of a hammer. He didn't need to look to know it was the Spencer, or who had scooped it up while he was preoccupied with the Apaches.

"The boot is on the other foot now, hoss," Burt Raidler said. "I want you to drop your rifle and shuck that pistol, and do it real slow. I'd rather not blow a hole in you, but by God I will if you try anything."

Gwen Pearson had been watching the Apache flee. "Burt! You wouldn't!" she exclaimed, taking a step.

"That's far enough!" the Texan warned. "I don't know whose side you're on. But I ain't about to trust you, seein' as how you didn't raise a fuss when he took my shootin' iron."

Gwen stamped a foot. "Sakes alive, but you two get my

goat! Why are men so pigheaded? We should be working together, not against one another. More Apaches could be close
by. Skye needs his guns."

"If we're attacked I'll give them back. Not before." Raidler prodded Fargo. "Now do as I told you, mister, and no one
has to be hurt."

Frowning, Fargo lowered the Henry until the stock rested
on the ground, then he let it fall. Using two fingers, he slowly
pulled the Colt and extended it behind him for the cowboy to
take. "Here. I've got a pill under the hammer and I don't
want it to go off."

"I don't blame you," Raidler said, grasping the barrel.

For an instant the Texan's eyes were on the Colt and not
on Fargo. Whirling and swatting the Spencer in one lightning
move, Fargo slammed into Burt Raidler, tackling him around
the waist. The cowboy futilely tried to level the Spencer but
by then he was flat on his back and Fargo had pressed the
Colt against his cheek.

"Damn, you're a clever cuss!" Raidler said, not batting an
eye at having a revolver shoved in his face.

Fargo slowly straightened, lowered the Colt, and twirled it
into his holster. "You can keep your hardware."

Raidler looked as if he had just swallowed a scorpion,
whole. "Are you addlepated? Make up your mind. A minute
ago you were ready to shoot me if I so much as touched a
gun. Now I can keep 'em?"

The lady from Missouri shared his confusion. "You sure
are fickle, Skye."

To Burt, Fargo said, "You could have shot me and didn't.
If you were the one who murdered Elias Hackman, you
wouldn't pass up the chance. Gwen and I are the only two
who know. You'd kill us to protect yourself."

"I suppose the killer would," Raidler agreed, sitting up.
"But you seem to have overlooked the fact I'm not the only
jasper who might have done it. There are eight other men
from that stage wanderin' around somewhere."

The cowboy didn't know. Fargo told him about the two

immigrants and the boy. About Buck Dawson being wounded. About the drummer taking the team to the oaks. Everything.

"I'm sure sorry to hear about Jones and those funny fellers. But if they're dead, and old Buck is bad hurt, and Virgil Tucker ain't anywhere near here, that leaves just one of us, don't it?"

"William Frazier the Third," Fargo said.

Gwen was skeptical. "What do you two use for brains? Oatmeal? He's the richest one of us all. He has more money than most of us will see in our lifetimes. Why would he stoop to stealing? You're both crazy as a peach-orchard boar."

"Maybe there's another white feller hereabouts," Raidler remarked. "Someone we don't know about."

It was Fargo's turn to be skeptical. No sane man would be traipsing around Apache country with a band of renegades on the warpath. "We'll find out soon enough," was his reply.

The Ovaro had arrived. Fargo stepped into the stirrups, then the Texan gave Gwen a hand up. They headed for the grazing mule, Raidler blowing and brushing dust from the Spencer's magazine.

Fargo had been meaning to ask him a question. "What happened last night after you left the gully?"

"It was too ridiculous for words, pard. We followed the Apaches a spell but couldn't keep up with 'em. And we couldn't track 'em because it was too dark to see worth a hoot. I thought they had gone one way, Frazier thought they'd gone another, and Elias Hackman didn't give a damn one way or another. He wanted to go back. Kept sayin' as how we were all dead if we didn't." Raidler kicked a small rock. "I got tired of hearin' him jabber so I walked on ahead. I was thinkin' about the fix we're in, and how I'd rather be shot than ever take a stage again. And next thing I know, the greenhorns had up and vanished."

"They lost sight of you and went another way," Gwen said.

"I reckon, although all they had to do was give a holler and I'd have come runnin'."

"Did you yell for them?" Fargo asked.

"Well, no. I was afeared the Apaches would hear. But I searched all over. And when I was done, I was as lost as they were. I got so turned around, I couldn't be sure which way the gully was. So I just started walkin'." The Texan looked down at his well-worn boots. "I've walked more in the past twenty-four hours than I have in the past twenty-four years. Once I get me a new horse, I ain't ever gettin' off him. I'll eat in the saddle, sleep in the saddle, change clothes in the saddle. You name it."

Fargo laughed. "You didn't see any sign of the others until you found Hackman's body?"

"No, but I did hear some shots once and a lot of whoopin' and hollerin'. When the sun came up, I was as lost as lost could be. Then I stumbled on some footprints and followed 'em into that canyon where Hackman was lyin'. I didn't see anyone else. Once I found he was dead, I left. Headed south, hopin' to reach the road before old age set in."

"Then we came along," Gwen interjected.

"Yes, ma'am. And I apologize again for takin' those shots at you. I was worn to a frazzle, so tired I couldn't see straight. And with the sun in my eyes and all—"

"We don't hold it against you," Fargo said.

"Still, what I did was terrible. I know better than to shoot unless I'm sure what I'm aimin' at. If I'd shot either of you, I wouldn't be able to live with myself. I'm a puncher, not a man-killer."

There was no denying the Texan's sincerity. Fargo no longer distrusted him, even a little. "I'll take Gwen and you to the others," he said. Then what? Should he go after William Frazier III? Or get everyone else out of there while he could? Before something else happened and more lives were lost?

"I sure will have some exciting stories to tell my kin in California," Gwen mentioned. "Nothing like this has ever happened to anyone in my family."

Raidler arched an eyebrow. "Your notion of excitement

and mine are two different things, ma'am. Lordy. You must be one of those who likes to read those trashy dime novels."

At the mention, Fargo could not help scowling. About a year ago, back East, a writer had come out with the first of what were now known as dime novels. Short stories, crammed with thrilling adventures. And hardly two words in any tale were true. The writers made up whatever struck their fancy, inventing characters out of whole cloth. The novels were very popular. Incredibly, many readers took them as gospel. Easterners got so caught up in the exploits of their favorite characters, they wanted to be just like them.

Several writers had tried to get Fargo to sit down and relate his life's story so they could do a series of novels. Friends of his, fellow scouts and lawmen, had done just that and had regretted it afterward. Facts were always changed to suit the writer's whim. As a scout at Fort Laramie put it, "My memory must be going. Beats me how I could forget I wrestled grizzlies, rode tornadoes, and wiped out half the Blackfeet."

Now, climbing out of the arroyo, Fargo saw the mule had drifted closer. It raised its head but didn't run off. Talking softly, Burt Raidler was able to get near enough to grab the bridle. He mounted, then said, "I'm glad none of my pards back home can see me. They'd laugh themselves to death."

"Whatever for?" Gwen asked.

"A puncher ain't a puncher unless he's on a horse." Raidler hefted the reins. "I might as well be on a sow as this critter."

Fargo turned to the south. He was anxious to check on Melissa Starr and the others. If Tucker had reached the oaks safely, they could be on their way before sunset. But as he kneed the stallion, he glanced to the west. Cresting a ridge were eight riders. They were too far away to note their features but he could see headbands on every one. "Apaches."

Gwen dug her nails into his sides. "What do we do?"

"We ride like hell."

Fargo galloped off. He couldn't go as fast as he would like

thanks to the mule. It was no match for the stallion, and Fargo was not about to race off and leave the Texan behind.

Yipping and yowling, the Apache swept down from the ridge. They were on mules, too. Apparently they had spared some of the animals that once belonged to the freighters.

Ten minutes of pursuit resulted in Fargo and Raidler pulling further and further ahead. The Apaches didn't give up, though. They forged on with the persistence of bulldogs, pacing themselves, maybe in the hope that the pinto or Raidler's mule would tire and they could catch up.

Landmarks to the west let Fargo know they were near the road. Another mile, he figured. They would be close to the oaks, too, which he didn't like. He had to lead the Apaches away from Melissa and Dawson, not toward them. "I say we go east a ways to throw the Apaches off the scent. Once we lose them, we'll backtrack."

"It's okay by me," Raidler said. "But this mule is actin' up."

Fargo had seen it balk a few times. The Texan had to keep lashing the reins and smacking it with his legs. The farther they went, the worse the mule acted. Fargo had no choice but to slow to a trot, then a walk. Meanwhile, the Apaches came closer and closer.

"We have to do something," Gwen said, stating the obvious.

Raidler raked his spurs across the mule's side but the stubborn animal refused to go any faster. "I might as well be ridin' a turtle."

So much for Fargo's plan. He pointed at a low hill covered by boulders. "Head there! We'll make a stand."

"Not on your life," the cowboy said. "Take Miss Pearson and light a shuck. You can still get away. Don't worry about me."

"We're not leaving you," Fargo said.

"Then you're a blamed fool. She's more important."

A stone's throw from the hill, the mule stopped dead and refused to take another step. The Texan got off, seized the bridle, and pulled and pulled. But the mule laid back its ears, dug in its hooves, and would not be budged. "You're worse than a jackass, you know that?" Raidler rasped in disgust.

They had a couple of minutes before the Apaches caught up. Sliding down, Fargo walked the last twenty yards at the cowboy's side. Some of the boulders were huge, some no bigger than a strongbox. He left Raidler to keep watch and climbed to an open space ringed by enough boulders to afford protection from stray bullets. "You'll be safer here than with us," he told Gwen.

To Fargo's surprise, the girl from Missouri threw her slender arms around him and held him close, saying in his ear, "Take care, you hear? I'm growing right fond of you." She added as an afterthought, "And Burt." Then she shyly pecked him on the cheek.

Fargo gave her the Colt. "If I hear a shot, I'll come running. Just don't shoot me by mistake."

Gwen tried to make light of their plight. "I'm not like that silly Texan. I won't fire unless I can see the whites of an Apache's eyes."

From down the hill Raidler bawled, "Here the varmints come!"

The warriors had spread out in a crescent moon formation and were almost within rifle range. They weren't in any particular hurry to lock horns. Fargo was almost to the bottom before it dawned on him why. He counted them and declared, "One's missing. There are only seven now."

Burt was crouched beside a boulder. "Three guesses where he got to."

"He's gone for help." Fargo thought he saw a horse and rider to the northwest but the heat haze distorted objects, so it might just be a tree. Crouching, he sighted on the center Apache, a stocky man with a blue headband. As soon as the warrior came within range, he would cut the odds even more.

"You should have taken the woman and skedaddled," Burt complained. "If she's harmed, I'll blame you."

"I'll blame me, too," Fargo confessed.

The Apaches halted just out of rifle shot. As safe as could be. Three slid off their mounts while two angled to the right, two to the left. They were going to ring the hill to prevent anyone from escaping.

Burt Raidler swore. "Looks like we've outsmarted ourselves. Got any new brainstorms? Because if not, we're goners."

Fargo refused to give up hope. Everything depended on how far away Chipota and the rest of the band were. "I'll be right back," he said, and retraced his steps up the hill, this time going past the nook where Gwen was hidden. From the summit he watched the four Apaches position themselves at fifty-yard intervals. Three had the presence of mind to stay out of range but the fourth was careless. Fargo swiftly descended.

The Texan was curious. "What did you see from up there? A patrol from Fort Breckinridge, I hope."

"We'll wait five minutes to make them think we've settled in, then we're making a break for it."

"Before the sun goes down?" the cowpuncher scoffed. "How far do you think we'll get?"

"A lot farther than if we don't try," Fargo said. They couldn't wait for dark to fall. It was six or seven hours off. By then Chipota might show up with enough warriors to wipe out a company of the Fifth Cavalry. He saw the mule Raidler had ridden mosey toward the Apaches, who displayed no interest in it.

"I still say you should take that gal and go. I can keep these fellers busy." Raidler grinned. "I promise not to die until you're out of sight."

"It wouldn't work."

The Texan quoted a saying common in the Pecos region. "Like a cow, I can try. And I don't see what we have to lose."

"Other than your life?"

"Damn, Fargo. You're as cantankerous as that uppity mule. It's worth it if we save Miss Pearson. Her life counts for more than both of ours combined."

Fargo tended to agree, but it wasn't in his nature to desert anyone in a time of need. They would all get out of there alive or none of them would. The Apaches had dismounted and squatted to await the arrival of reinforcements. So superbly were they conditioned, they could squat like that the rest of the day and the whole night through, if need be. Despite their warlike ways, Fargo had grudging respect for their prowess. And their streak of independence. They refused to bow under to anyone, not the Spaniards, not the Mexicans, not the American government. A love of freedom was a trait Fargo shared.

The minutes went by swiftly. Fargo scanned the horizon, then beckoned the Texan and crept up through the boulders. Gwen was rocking on her heels, the pistol trained on the opening. As his shadow fell across it, she jumped, relaxing when Fargo said, "It's only us. Time to leave."

"Where did the Apaches get to?"

"Nowhere," Raidler answered. "Fargo is fixin' to invite 'em up for cups of tea. While they're guzzlin' it, we'll sneak off."

"Pay no attention to him," Fargo advised. "He thinks he has a sense of humor." Leading the Ovaro, he picked a path to the northwest with the utmost care. They couldn't afford for the Apaches to spot the stallion. By a circuitous route, always keeping the pinto behind the biggest of boulders, he reached the point he wanted, near the base of the hill and as close as he could get to the one warrior within rifle range.

"Let me guess," Burt Raidler said. "We're going to break through these red demons and into those trees yonder?"

"That's the general idea." Fargo put his hands on Gwen's hips and effortlessly swung her onto the saddle. "Bend low and stay low. Once the shooting starts, we've got to reach that mule"—he pointed—"as quickly as we can."

"If it doesn't run off," Raidler said. "And what about the other braves while all this is going on? Think they'll just sit there and let us ride away? Maybe wave and give us their blessin'?"

The warrior was watching a hawk pinwheel high overhead. Fargo leaned on a boulder, used it as a rifle rest, and centered the front sight on the Apache's chest. Lining up the rear sight, he compensated for the distance by raising the barrel a fraction. Wind wasn't a factor, as it had died down.

"Are you sure you can hit him from here?" Gwen asked. "It's an awful long shot."

"I couldn't," Raidler said.

Fargo inhaled and held it. He had to be rock steady when he fired. Seconds trickled by like grains of sand from an hourglass. The warrior lost interest in the hawk and stared at the hill. Fargo's whole body imitated marble. His finger curled ever so slowly. The boom of the Henry was amplified by the closely packed boulders, his ears ringing as the sound rumbled off across the wasteland.

The Apache pitched onto his face, convulsing.

"Now!" Fargo said, running into the open. Gwen was at his elbow, the cowboy on the other side of the stallion. Yells erupted as Apaches who had not seen the warrior fall demanded to know what had happened from those who did. Those nearest leaped to their mules and mounted. The next warrior on the right was already rushing to intercept them but two swift shots from the Texan's Spencer made him swerve aside.

The mule belonging to the dead man began to stray off, its reins trailing.

Fargo quickened the pace. They needed that animal, at all costs. Losing it would be a calamity, requiring one of them to stay behind to face certain death. He banged a round at the Apache on the left, who chose the wiser part of valor and retreated. But more warriors were streaking around the hill.

The mule lumbered into a trot.

"No!" Gwen cried.

Fargo spun and vaulted onto the saddle. A prod of his heels was sufficient. As always, the stallion lit out like a bat out of hell.

Gwen gripped his shoulders. "What are you going? What about Burt? We can't just leave him!"

Fargo didn't have time to explain. He glanced back. The two groups of Apaches were advancing again, but cautiously. Burt Raidler appeared stunned. Then he grinned and waved, fed a bullet into the Spencer, and faced the group to the southwest, prepared to sell his life dearly.

It wouldn't come to that if Fargo had any say. He saw the mule come to a grassy tract and stop to graze. It raised its head as the pinto bore down, but it didn't flee. In another few seconds Fargo hauled on the Ovaro's reins, slowing just enough so he could grab the mule's. A sharp wrench, and they were flying back toward the Texan.

Gwen, in her excitement, pounded on Fargo's shoulders. "Go! Go! Don't let them do him in!"

The three Apaches to the east were closest. Fargo snapped off a shot to deter them. What with the barrel bouncing and bobbing, he didn't expect to hit one. So he was all the more pleased when the foremost flung both arms out and fell.

Fargo was halfway there. The mule picked that moment to resist by jerking its head back. But Fargo was not to be denied. The reins were wrapped securely around his wrist. He yanked on them hard enough to rip the bit from the mule's mouth.

"Burt! Burt!" Gwen bawled. "Here we come!"

The Texan was firing at the Apaches on the right, keeping them at bay. Hearing her shout, he swiveled and showed more teeth than a politician stumping for votes. Raidler backpedaled, squeezed a final shot at the Apaches, then sprinted to meet them.

Lead sizzled past Fargo's ear. The warrior who had fired was next to another armed with a bow. Bending it nearly in half, the archer let a shaft fly. Fargo followed its flight. He saw it arc up, saw the barbed tip glitter in the sunlight. Then it arced down—straight at Burt Raidler.

9

Skye Fargo opened his mouth to shout a warning but Gwen Pearson beat him to it. She bent forward, her mouth next to his ear, and screeched at the top of her lungs. It felt as if she nearly shattered his eardrum. Pain lanced Fargo's skull like a red-hot knife.

"Burt! Look out! Above you!"

Raidler heard her even above the booming of his Spencer, and tilted his head back. Then, with barely an instant to spare, he threw himself to the left. The arrow thudded into the exact spot where he had been standing, imbedding itself four or five inches. Raidler landed on his knees but he was immediately up again, and running.

Fargo fired at an Apache looping toward them from the east. He missed, but he came close because the warrior veered off. In another few moments they reached the Texan and Raidler swung up onto the mule.

"Head for the trees!" Fargo directed, doing likewise.

Between the Henry and the Spencer, they kept the Apaches from getting too close, their rifles thundering in steady cadence. Several arrows rained down, one almost transfixing the mule's neck.

"We did it!" Gwen exclaimed as they sped into the undergrowth. "They won't dare follow us because they know we'll pick them off!"

Her opinion of Apaches could stand correcting but Fargo didn't enlighten her. Reining up, he saw that the Apaches had regrouped and halted. Five were left. One appeared to be wounded and was slumped over. Fargo quickly dismounted and gave the reins to Gwen. "Stay on," he told her.

Raidler slid down and handed the mule's reins up, as well.

"What are you going to do?" Gwen asked.

"They can't see us at the moment. Burt and I will stay here while you ride off." Fargo nodded to the north. "Go slowly, and cross that clearing up ahead. On the other side stop and wait for us."

The cowboy smirked. "Oh, I get it. I bet you're a hellion at checkers."

Gwen protested. "I don't want to leave you."

"Just do it," Fargo said. "Hurry, while they're just sitting there."

Grumbling, Gwen flapped her arms and legs. "All right. All right. Hold your britches on." She moved deeper into the brush, the mule in tow.

Crouching, Fargo glided to the edge of the trees. He was careful not to expose himself. Coming to a wide trunk, he sank to one knee, removed his hat, and peered out. The Apaches had not moved. Several were arguing. Another suddenly straightened and stared at the vegetation, then said something that put an end to the spat. Fargo glanced back. Gwen was crossing the clearing. From where the Apaches were, they wouldn't be able to tell she was alone. "Get set," he whispered.

"It'll be like shootin' ducks in a barrel."

"We can't leave any alive," Fargo said grimly. Not if they wanted to make a clean escape. So long as one warrior lived to shadow them and mark their trail for Chipota, they were in deadly peril.

"No complaints here, pard," Raidler said. "I ain't one of those who thinks the only good injun is a dead injun. Had me a Cherokee friend once, and he'd do to ride the river with any day. But with Apaches I'd gladly make an exception."

It was a sentiment shared by many otherwise peaceable people. Apache depredations had so enraged the citizens of Arizona, they wouldn't mind if every last one was rounded up and executed, or shipped to a federal reservation in Florida. Which, to an Apache, would be the same as a death sentence. Apaches didn't fare well on reservations. They were warriors, not farmers. And those thrown into prison fared even worse. They couldn't stand to be cooped up behind high walls. Like plants denied the sun, they withered and died. And nary a tear was shed by the whites who put them there.

Fargo saw four of the renegades move toward the trees. The fifth man, the wounded warrior, had wheeled his mount and was riding to the west. Already he was out of range. The only way to stop him would be to go after him.

"Here they come!" Raidler said excitedly.

The quartet were in a knot. They were in no great hurry. They figured to follow at a discreet distance, keeping track of their quarry until Chipota came. That was Fargo's guess, anyway. He aimed at the burly archer who had nearly killed the cowboy. "Wait until they're right on top of us. Don't shoot until I do."

"We should get a gun or two for Miss Pearson."

A good idea, Fargo reflected, but they shouldn't put the cart before the horse. He was as still as the tree, watching their eyes, particularly those of the two in front. Their eyes would give them away if they spotted Raidler or him.

Crackling in the brush had ceased. Gwen had reined up to await the outcome. Fargo hoped she did exactly as he instructed her. If she had turned around and was sneaking back to see what happened, she could spoil everything.

The four warriors were now less than thirty yards out. As vigilant as wolves, they scoured the trees. An old-timer once told Fargo that taking an Apache by surprise was asking a miracle of the Almighty. "They can hear a pin drop from fifty paces. They can hunt by scent, just like bloodhounds. And they can see like an eagle. No one ever takes Apaches unawares."

The oldster had exaggerated, but not by much. Fargo saw the warrior with the bow tense, his dark eyes never at rest, as if he sensed something was wrong but could not quite pinpoint it.

Twenty-five yards away the quartet slowed. All of them were ramrod straight, fully alert. The archer was studying the tree line.

Fargo resisted an urge to fire. They had to be closer, so close none could get away. He focused on the bowman, whose gaze had roved to the left and was slowly sweeping across the greenery. Fargo saw the man look right at the tree he was behind, then sweep past. Suddenly the warrior's eyes darted back again. They widened in surprise. The time had come.

At the blast of the Henry, the archer was flipped backward as if punched by a giant. A second later Raidler's Spencer cracked and a second Apache went down. The remaining two reacted differently. One whipped a rifle up, the other turned his mule, hugged its back, and fled.

A slug thumped into the trunk a hand's-width from Fargo. He banged off a shot, heard Raidler echo him. The Apache with the rifle was lifted clean off his mount to sprawl beside the bowman.

Fargo dashed from concealment for a better shot at the one who was fleeing. He had to aim carefully or he would hit the mule. Then Raidler's rifle spoke, and the animal's front knees caved in. The Apache flew clear as the mule crashed down. Rising, the man raced for the hill, weaving and bounding like a jackrabbit. Fargo tried to fix a bead but the warrior zigzagged too erratically. Raidler squeezed off two shots that had no effect.

Fargo adopted a new tactic. He trained the Henry on thin air a dozen feet to the right of the warrior, then waited. The Apache angled right, angled left, angled right again, moving a little farther each time. Abruptly, the man's back filled the Henry's sights, and Fargo fired.

The impact smashed the warrior onto his belly. He clawed briefly at the dirt, cried out, and died.

"Damn, you're good," Burt Raidler said.

The fifth Apache, the wounded one, had witnessed the death of his fellows. He didn't linger. The mule raised puffs of dust as it sped off.

Fargo lowered the Henry. By the time he ran to the Ovaro and gave chase, the warrior would have a considerable lead. Eventually the stallion would overtake him, but by then they would be miles away, maybe within earshot of Chipota.

Raidler was bent over a dead warrior, stripping the man of a pistol, rifle, and cartridge belt. "These should do Miss Pearson. Too bad they don't have any food with 'em."

The reminder made Fargo's stomach growl. When the cowboy was done, they jogged into the woods. Gwen was right where she was supposed to be. She gave the Texan a fleeting hug, then warmly embraced Fargo, her breath warm on his ear.

"I'm losing count of how many times you've saved my life now. Keep making a habit of it and I don't know how I'll ever repay you."

Fargo looked her right in the eyes. "I can think of a way."

The lady from Missouri blushed from her throat to her hairline, then puckered her mouth as if sucking on a cherry and gave him an inviting wink. Only Fargo saw. Raidler was busy reloading.

Gwen scooted to the pinto and gripped the saddle horn. "Now we can head for those oaks you told us about, right?"

"Wrong," Fargo said.

"What? Why on earth not?"

Raidler looked at her. "I reckon I know, ma'am. One of those varmints got away. More will come along before too long."

"So? We'll be far away by then."

"Not far enough," Fargo said. "Apaches are some of the best trackers in the world. We'd lead them right to Melissa, Buck, and Tucker. Is that what you want?"

Gwen's spirits sagged and so did she, against the stallion. The long hours without sleep, with no food, the constant danger, were taking a toll. Their trial had turned the fresh-faced country girl into a pale shadow of her former self. "Lord, I don't know how much more of this I can take. What are we going to do, then?"

Fargo opened a saddlebag to take out spare ammunition. "Lose the Apaches."

"Is that possible? When they can track as well as you can?"

"I've been through this region before. I know of a table-land to the north where the ground is as hard as iron. Solid rock in some places. We won't be able to completely erase our tracks but we can slow the Apaches down. Buy us a day, maybe two."

"Is it far, this tableland?"

"Seven miles as the crow flies."

Gwen halfheartedly swiped a hand at her hair. "More riding. Just what I need." She pulled herself up. "I never thought I would say this, as much as I love horses. But I can't wait to be in that nice, comfortable stage, on my way to California."

"You will be, soon enough," Fargo said. But it was one thing to make such a promise and another to keep it. Chipota would crave revenge after losing so many men and would hound them ruthlessly. Chipota had to. The losses would bother his followers. They'd begin to think that maybe Chipota had lost some of his medicine, that maybe he wasn't the great leader he styled himself to be. To prove he was fit to lead, to keep his band intact, Chipota must slay those who had slain his warriors.

With all that had happened, Fargo had lost track of time. It mildly surprised him to learn the sun was high in the afternoon sky. He also noticed the Ovaro beginning to flag soon after they headed out. From then on he held to a walk.

In an hour or so they came to a ribbon of a stream, the water barely four inches deep. Yet to them and the animals it was a godsend. Moving stiffly, Fargo lowered onto his stomach and drank greedily. He wanted to go on gulping until he couldn't swallow another drop, but he contended himself with splashing water on his neck and face and letting some trickle under his shirt.

Gwen was wet from her hair to her shoulders. Laughing merrily, she cupped a handful and poured it down the front of her dress. "Ahhh! If I were alone, I'd strip and lie here until I was as shriveled as a prune."

Raidler chuckled. "Shucks. Don't let us stop you."

Fargo was anxious to go on but he let Gwen frolic awhile. It did wonders for her mood and perked all of them up. The pinto and the mule also had their vitality restored. But it would be short-lived, Fargo knew, without rest and food. When they resumed riding he was on the lookout for something to shoot for supper but few creatures were ever abroad during the hottest part of the day.

Vegetation became sparse. The ground became rocky. To reach the tableland they had to negotiate a switchback. From their new vantage point they could see twice as far along their back trail.

"Do you see what I see?" Raidler asked.

"Oh, no," Gwen said. "Not this soon."

A column of dust swirled about a group of riders. Fargo wished he had a spyglass. Not that he needed one. It had to be Chipota's band, two hours back, no more. He struck off across the tableland, selecting the rockiest stretches, relying on his considerable skill to leave sign so faint even an Apache would be stymied. Above, the sun was a glowing inferno that scorched the land and blistered them, sucking the moisture from their bodies, making them worse off than they were before they found the stream.

Sweat poured from Fargo's pores. It got into his eyes, stinging them. Wiping his sleeve across his face was little help since two minutes later he was just as sweaty. Gwen sat propped against him, fitfully napping. Every now and then she would mumble to herself. The Texan had his big hat pulled low and rode as limply as a scarecrow.

The Apaches would find them easy pickings.

Fargo willed himself to go on. Even when the heat sapped

almost all his energy, even when he could barely lift an arm or keep his eyes open. In due course they came to a gravel-strewn slope that linked the tableland to a series of canyons.

Gwen stirred, saying thickly, "I can't go much further, Skye. We need to rest. Please."

"Soon," Fargo said.

Gravel slid out from under their mounts, cascading below them. The Ovaro slipped but regained its balance. The mule slipped, and didn't. Burt Raidler lurched and would have fallen had he not gripped its neck. Legs pumping, the mule sought to stay upright, its efforts dislodging more and more gravel. It stumbled, then gravity took over.

"Roll clear!" Fargo shouted.

The Texan had the same idea. Pushing off, he saved his leg from being pinned. But when he tried to scramble erect, the treacherous footing hindered him. He was only halfway up when the mule slid into him and bowled him over. Both were swept toward the bottom by the increasing avalanche of loose stones and earth.

Gwen had awakened. "Hurry! Help him! He'll be hurt!"

Fargo would have liked nothing better than to help, but he dared not spur the Ovaro or they would suffer the same mishap. Legs taut against the stirrups, he carefully descended, stopping whenever the gravel threatened to give way.

Stones rattling, dirt spewing, the mule kept on sliding until it was at the bottom. Raidler clung to its neck, the lower half of his body underneath the animal, the Spencer and his hat gone. When the mule came to a stop, they both struggled to stand, Raidler crying out when he applied weight to his legs. The mule shook itself, its coat marred by cuts and abrasions.

"What's wrong with Burt?" Gwen asked.

Once on solid ground, Fargo dropped from the saddle and rushed to the Texan's side. The cowboy had staggered to a flat boulder and was lying across it, eyes shut, face contorted in a grimace. "How bad is it?" Fargo asked.

Raidler grunted. "My left leg feels like a bull stomped on it."

Gwen helped Fargo roll him over. Fargo started to hike Raidler's pants but Raidler grit his teeth and sputtered in torment. Drawing the Arkansas toothpick, Fargo stooped to press it against the cowboy's jeans.

"What do you think you're doing?"

Fargo thought it should be obvious. "We need to cut your pants."

"Like hell. They cost me fourteen dollars, cash money. And money doesn't grow on trees." Huffing and puffing, Raidler sat up. "Have Miss Pearson turn around and I'll pull 'em down."

"I've seen naked men before," Gwen declared.

Something told Fargo that if she had, it wasn't very many. He motioned and she pivoted, folding her arms.

Raidler fumbled at his belt, hissing in frustration when his fingers couldn't do as he wanted. Swaying, he swore softly and tried again. The blood drained from his face and a groan escaped him. "I can do it," he said, bitter at his failure. "I know I can. Just give me a couple of minutes to catch my breath."

"We don't have the time to spare," Fargo responded. A surge of his shoulders and the razor-sharp toothpick slit the pants leg from above the boot to below the knee. Raidler squawked but the damage had been done. Fargo widened the opening, half fearing he would find shattered bone jutting from ruptured skin. The leg appeared to be undamaged. But when he put a hand on the shin, Raidler yelped like a stricken coyote.

"Damn! What did you do?"

"I just touched you." Fargo probed along the bone.

Another cry was torn from the Texan's throat. Raidler collapsed on his back, a forearm over his eyes, his chest heaving. "Lawsy! I haven't hurt this bad since I was ten and had a bellyache from eatin' a bucket of green apples."

"I think it's fractured."

"With the run of luck I've been having, what else did you expect? I must have had a bad case of the simples when I bought that stage ticket. I'd have been better off shootin' myself."

Fargo uncurled. "We need a splint but there aren't any trees handy."

Raidler chortled, then said bitterly, "Of course not. It's what I get for not having the brains God gave a squirrel. My ma was right. I should've been a clerk instead of a cowpuncher. Pushin' papers is a might borin', but at least when they fall on you, they don't bust bones."

Nudging Gwen, Fargo said, "Give me a hand. We have to get him on the mule."

The Texan moaned. "I'd rather you just leave me."

"Will you quit joshing?" the blonde bantered. "A big, strapping man like you shouldn't let a little thing like a broken leg make a crybaby out of him."

"A crybaby?" Raidler repeated, his dander up. "Those are fightin' words in the Pecos country, ma'am. I'll prove to you I'm as much a man as the next fella." Suddenly sliding off the boulder, he pushed to his feet on his own. And promptly paid for it by going as white as a sheet and keeling forward.

A quick bound, and Fargo caught the cowboy before he hit the ground. "I'm surprised you've lived as long as you have," he joked, but Raidler was in no condition to appreciate the humor.

"Hit me over the noggin with a big rock. That ought to stop the torture."

Fargo regarded the mule a moment. There was no easy way to do it, no way to spare the cowboy tremendous agony. "Gwen, take his other side." They locked eyes as she obeyed. "On the count of three," Fargo said, and Gwen nodded.

Raidler gripped their shoulders. "Lord, have mercy," he breathed.

It would have gone well except Gwen's grip slipped as they were swinging Raidler up and over. His body tilted, his fractured leg hit the mule, and he barely stifled a scream, his face so red he looked ready to burst a vein. Fargo slipped both arms under the Texan's chest and pushed. Like a schoolyard seesaw, Raidler teetered upward and roosted on the mule's back, his good leg over the side but his damaged leg as limp as a wet rag. Fargo lowered it, being as gentle as he could.

"There," Gwen said. "That wasn't so hard, was it?"

The Texan looked at her as if she were loco. "No," he croaked. "I could do it once a day and twice on Sunday." He rolled his eyes, his arms dangling.

"Why do men always fall apart over a little pain?" Gwen asked Fargo. "My ma used to say that every man is a baby in bigger clothes. Why, if men had to give birth to real babies, like we do, there wouldn't be another child born. You couldn't take labor and all we go through."

Fargo had heard the same argument from other women, and he had the same answer for her that he gave the others. "It all balances out. Women have to put up with the pain of giving birth, and men have to put up with women bragging about how tough it is."

"Typical man," Gwen huffed.

"I'm all male and proud of it."

"That wasn't what I meant and you know it."

To nip her indignation in the bud, Fargo suggested they search for the Spencer and the Texan's hat. Five minutes of cautious prowling turned up the latter but not the rifle. Buried, Fargo reckoned, under the small avalanche.

They couldn't spare any more time. Fargo forked leather once more. Gwen clambered up behind him, wrapped her arms around his middle, and pressed against him so tight he could feel her breasts mash against his back. He wondered if it was her way of hinting her interest hadn't waned.

Fargo rode to the southeast. They needed water, they needed rest. Most of all, they needed to fix a splint for Raidler or infection might set in. Fargo had seen it happen once to a man with a busted arm even though the bone never broke the skin. With the nearest sawbones hundreds of miles away, Raidler would be as good as dead.

The rocks, the boulders, the ground itself gave off heat in stifling waves. Fatigue set in again. Combined with the wounds and bruises Fargo had suffered, his body felt as if he had been caught in a buffalo stampede. When—or rather, *if*—he made it out of Arizona alive, he would treat himself to two or three days at a fine hotel. He'd sleep in every day until noon, soak in a bath for hours, then visit the best saloons in town. A few nights of drinking, of gambling and carousing to all hours, of generally raising hell for the sheer hell of it, would do more good than a month of bedrest. He could hardly wait.

A stand of cottonwoods seemed out of place on the arid plain. Cottonwoods thrived near water, so Fargo thought they might find a spring. But any water was underground. He dug a few holes without striking moisture.

To make a splint, Fargo trimmed a pair of fallen limbs, then cut whangs from his buckskins and knotted them together. Raidler was unconscious but he roused when he was lowered to the grass.

"Leave me be. I want to die in peace."

"Oh, shush," Gwen said. "You're talking crazy. My ma used to say that orneriness adds years to a person's life. If that's the case, you should live to be a hundred."

Raidler had trouble keeping his eyes open. "Your ma said a lot of things, didn't she?"

"She was a wise woman."

The cowboy smirked. "She ever say you look like a chipmunk with those high cheeks and button nose? You flap your gums like one, too."

"Why, that's plain rude," Gwen declared. "My ma also said to never marry a Texan. Now I know why." But Raidler wasn't listening. He had passed out.

From there they rode south, Fargo's knack for judging the lay of the land serving them in good stead. They came to the same stream they had stopped at earlier, only well to the east.

As thirsty as he was, before he drank Fargo climbed a tree and surveyed the parched landscape they had crossed. No tendrils of dust were visible.

"Did we do it?" Gwen asked when he knelt beside her. "Did we give them the slip?"

"Time will tell."

Half an hour's rest was all Fargo would allow. They pressed on, and shortly before sunset they spied the road. Tears of happiness welled up in Gwen's eyes as she hugged Fargo and kissed him on the neck.

"Thank God! We're safe at last!"

In Apache territory no one was ever safe. Fargo twisted to say so, then abruptly drew rein and clamped a hand over her mouth.

Approaching from the west were five men on horseback.

10

Skye Fargo's first thought was that they were Apaches. It was logical to assume, what with the region crawling with Chipota's band. He removed his hand from Gwen and went to rein the Ovaro around before the warriors spotted them, then paused when he realized that instead of wearing headbands and loincloths, the five men wore *uniforms.* Blue uniforms so caked by dust they appeared to be gray. But there was no mistaking their distinctive caps, their buttons, their insignia.

"They're soldiers!" Gwen Pearson breathed. Then, waving her arms, she hollered, "Over here! We need help! We're white people!"

One of the troopers elevated an arm and all five came to a stop. Fargo reined the stallion toward them, the mule plodding alongside. Burt Raidler was unconscious, a merciful state in light of how much torment he had suffered.

"We're saved!" Gwen exclaimed. Choked with emotion, she clasped Fargo and said it over and over again.

Fargo didn't disillusion her. Encountering the troopers was a stroke of luck but they were still in great danger. Five soldiers were no match for forty Apaches. But the troopers would be of great help in protecting the passengers still alive.

The insignia on the soldier who had brought the quintet to a stop identified him as a lieutenant. He was young, his chin as hairless as a baby's backside. Squaring his shoulders, he formally announced, "Lieutenant Peter Jones, First Cavalry, at your service." Then he blinked. "Mr. Fargo? Is that you? I saw you at Fort Breckinridge, talking with Colonel Davenport."

Fargo couldn't recall seeing the junior officer before. There had been so many soldiers at the fort, though, he couldn't be expected to remember each and every face. "It's me. A lot the worse for wear." He introduced Gwen and explained about Raidler's leg.

"I don't understand," Lieutenant Jones said. "Where did these people come from? It was my understanding you were going to ride to the San Simon way station and leave word on whether you found any recent Apache sign." He gestured at the other troopers. "That's why we're here. Colonel Davenport sent us to visit the stage station and obtain any message you left."

So that was it. Fargo wished the colonel had sent an entire detachment. "I never made it to the station," he divulged, and told about his run-in with the stage, and Chipota being on the prowl.

"My word," the lieutenant said. "You've been through sheer hell. But rest easy now. My men and I will see to it that the passengers are escorted safely to the fort."

"Have you ever fought Apaches before?" Fargo asked.

"Well, no, sir, I haven't. But I've heard all about them, and I'm eager to test my mettle. Colonel Davenport ordered me to avoid engaging them, if at all possible. But if not, then to uphold the honor of the First Cavalry to the best of my ability."

"Davenport is a wise man," Fargo commented. Which was more than he could say about Jones. The lieutenant was so green, it was a wonder he didn't have clover sprouting from his ears. "Testing his mettle," as Jones had phrased it, was the last thing they needed. Still, Fargo wasn't going to refuse whatever help the officer rendered. "The spot where I left the others is about two miles east of here. We can be there before the sun goes down."

"Excellent." Lieutenant Jones turned in the saddle. "You

heard the man. Effective immediately, our first priority is to protect these civilians."

On the officer's right was an older trooper whose chevrons denoted he was a sergeant. "Begging the lieutenant's pardon, sir," he said. "But after what Mr. Fargo just told, is it wise to head for the post? It might be safer to go on to the San Simon and wait for a patrol to come by."

"Nonsense, Sergeant Myers. Did we see any Apaches when we came through the gorge? No. Have we seen any since? No. They're long gone, in my estimation." Lieutenant Jones gave Myers a patronizing smile. "I know the colonel sent you along to keep an eye on me, Sergeant. To see I don't make any mistakes. You needn't worry. I'll get us all to the fort in one piece."

The noncom held his peace but his sentiments were mirrored in his eyes, and Fargo shared them. The officer was too young, too raw, too cocksure of himself. Fargo agreed they should head for the station and mulled over how best to convince Jones as they headed out.

"I must say," the lieutenant commented. "This is quite an honor. Ever since I arrived in the West, I've been hearing stories about you, Mr. Fargo. Seeing you at the fort was a thrill. But to meet you in person—"

"I put on my boots one foot at a time, same as any man."

Lieutenant Jones cackled as if it were the funniest joke he'd ever heard. "I know, I know. But still, you're well on your way to becoming a legend. You've explored more of the West than I'll ever see, done things most men only dream of doing. I think I speak for many when I say that I envy you beyond measure."

Fargo stared at him, and damn if the boy wasn't sincere. "If you think that highly of me, maybe you'll take my advice."

"Sure. Anything. I'd bow to your seasoned judgment any day."

"Then do as the sergeant suggested and take the passengers to the San Simon." Jones opened his mouth to respond but Fargo held up a hand. "I know you'd rather go to the fort. I know you didn't see any Apaches on your way here. But they're out there, Lieutenant. Trust me. Some might be spying on us even as we speak."

"I don't want anyone to accuse me of cowardice," the officer said.

"Where did you ever get the idea anyone would?" Fargo thought of another point. "I know your colonel well. He likes to promote smart officers, not dead ones. And going to the station is smarter than trying to make it through the gorge with women and wounded men to look after."

Lieutenant Jones was cocky but he wasn't stupid. "I suppose you're right. Very well. The way station it is."

Fargo glanced at Sergeant Myers, who grinned and winked. His saddle creaked as Gwen shifted, then creaked again. Her arm poked him in the side. Curious as to what she was up to, Fargo looked over a shoulder.

Farm girls from Missouri and women from New York City had something in common. Both liked to be at their best when men were around. Gwen had smoothed her torn, dirty dress, wiped the dust from her face, and was running fingers through her hair to undo tangles. She had sat up straighter, too.

Fargo suppressed a chuckle. Some things never changed. The sun could burn out, the moon could fall, and men and women would go on doing the same silly things they had since the dawn of time.

Shortly, Burt Raidler muttered, opened his eyes, and slowly sat up. Groaning, he pressed a hand to his temple. "Dog my cats if there aren't longhorns jostlin' around in my skull. I feel all hot and light-headed." He raised his head. "I must be delirious. I'd swear I see five bluecoats."

"They're real enough," Gwen said. "You can relax now. The worst is over. We'll have you at a doctor before you can say Andrew Jackson."

"Good. Maybe I can swap this leg of mine for a new one. It feels as if a beaver is gnawing on it."

To the west the sun had dipped partly below the horizon, painting the sky with brilliant streaks of red, orange, and yellow. Arizona sunsets were spectacular. Soon the wind would change, bringing welcome relief from the stifling heat. Fargo removed his hat to mop his brow and tried not to dwell on the weariness that ate at his bones. And the Ovaro's. The stallion moved as if every step were an effort.

Lieutenant Jones coughed. "I was wondering, sir, whether you would see fit to share some of your more interesting experiences. For instance, they say you've lived among the Indians, and that no one knows them better than you do."

"I know we're in for a war one day that will make the Apache uprising seem tame."

"Sir?"

"People can only be pushed so far, Lieutenant. The white man has already driven the Indian from most land east of the Mississippi. There's talk of one day taking all the land west of the Mississippi, too. The Indians won't stand for it. More blood will be spilled then than in all the Indian wars so far."

"Times change, Mr. Fargo. People must change with it. What would you have us do? Still live along the East Coast? Never expand beyond thirteen colonies? We are an adventurous breed, and the lands in the West hold adventure and promise unlike any ever known."

Fargo had to concede the officer had a point. Maybe Jones wasn't as big a fool as he'd suspected.

"I saw that look when I mentioned fighting Apaches. But I'm a soldier, sir. Fighting is what I do. It is my key to advancement. And I fully intend to rise through the ranks, to one day be a general, to have command of the very army that will win that war you see coming." Lieutenant Jones smiled. "Seize life by the horns, I always say, and take what you may. Can you think of a better motto?"

The whiz of an arrow punctuated the statement. Lieutenant Jones gaped at the feathered end jutting from his chest, then turned his astonished gaze on Fargo. "My word," he said simply, then doubled over, dead before he hit the ground.

"Hostiles!" Sergeant Myers bellowed. "Open fire! Fire at will!"

From out of the high grass on both sides of the road they rose, over twenty Apaches, to unleash a volley of arrows and slugs. They had laid their trap well, waiting until the soldiers were at a point where retreat was impossible.

Fargo brought the Henry up and felled a husky warrior bearing down on him with a war club. He partly blamed himself for blundering into the ambush. Fatigue had dulled his senses. And he had compounded his neglect by paying more attention to Lieutenant Jones than their surroundings.

All the troopers were shooting. So was Gwen, the big Smith & Wesson dwarfing her hand. Even Burt Raidler joined in. But he was so weak, he could barely hold his pistol steady.

Fargo glanced both ways. They had to get out of there before they were slaughtered. There appeared to be more warriors to the south than to the north. Wheeling the pinto, Fargo yelled, "Follow me!" then resorted to his spurs, and yanked on the mule's reins.

When the animal broke into a trot, Raidler was nearly thrown. Bending, he succeeded in wrapping his arms around its neck.

"Hold on!" Gwen shouted.

Apache arrows and bullets zinged from all sides. Fargo thumbed off a shot, saw a warrior drop. Others were rushing to head them off. It would be close—very close.

Sergeant Myers bellowed for his men to follow. Keeping in close order, the four troopers gained the grass. Then a nine-foot war lance flashed, transfixing the chest of a soldier at the rear. From the other side streaked an arrow, cleaving the neck of another cavalryman. That left two, and two troopers weren't enough to stem the tide of red bloodlust.

Fargo looked back. The Apaches were concentrating on the soldiers, the enemies they hated the most. Were he alone, he would stand and fight by Myers's side. But Gwen and Raidler were dependent on him for their lives. It galled him, but he kept going.

Eight or nine Apaches swarmed over the remaining troopers. Sergeant Myers went down fighting, slaying two Apaches as he fell.

Suddenly a tall warrior loomed in front of the stallion. Fargo reined to the right and swept past. But the man wasn't interested in him. Or in Gwen. Before Fargo could guess his intent, the Apache took a few swift steps and sprang. Brawny hands closed on Burt Raidler's shirt and wrenched him off the mule.

"No!" Gwen shrieked. She punched Fargo on the shoulders. "Go back! Go back! Didn't you see!"

The trouble was, Fargo had seen. He also saw several more warriors converging, saw the mule seized, saw that if he turned around, he would be overwhelmed and none of them would escape alive. So he lashed the reins, never breaking the pinto's stride. Within moments they were in the clear.

Gwen was beside herself with outrage. "What are you doing? We have to save him! Turn around before it's too late!"

"It's already too late," Fargo answered.

"No!" Gwen put her hands on his lower back and started to slide off. "I'd rather die than run out on them!"

"Don't!" Fargo cried, reaching to grab her. She wouldn't listen. Pushing off, she dropped. It was a courageous but senseless gesture. She could no more save the soldiers or Raidler than she could stop the sun from setting. Yet if she wasn't using her head, was he any better? Fargo wondered as he spun the pinto on the head of a coin and rushed to save her from herself.

Gwen had bounced on her dainty bottom and was rubbing it as she stood. She seemed unaware that several amazed Apaches had witnessed her fall and were charging toward her.

Fargo was aware of them, though. He shot one through the chest, another through the shoulder. By then he was beside Gwen and he leaned down to grab her. Pigheaded to the end, she slapped his hand.

"I'm not going and that's final!"

Like hell it was! Fargo fumed. Vaulting down, he caught hold of her dress. When she tore loose, he lost all patience. He slugged her, full on the jaw, then swept her up by the waist and darted to the stallion. Throwing her over the saddle, he quickly clambered on. Two more Apaches were close but neither had a bow or rifle. One hurled a lance. The pinto was in motion by then and it missed by a wide margin.

Fargo gazed toward the road. Apaches were stripping the dead soldiers and mutilating the bodies. One had a tongue in his hand, waving the trophy proudly. Another was doing something to the lieutenant's face with a bowie knife.

Several warriors rose holding Burt Raidler between them. The Texan was still alive and apparently unharmed except for bruises and his leg. He hung limply as they carted him away.

Two cavalry mounts had run off. Two others had fallen into the hands of the war party, along with the mule. Fargo took it for granted they would give chase, and they did, but he was a quarter of a mile away by then. It helped that twilight soon fell. As the darkness deepened and the Apaches realized they had little hope of catching him, they gave up and turned back.

An hour after sunset Fargo brought them to the same stream they had visited twice already, to a belt of cottonwoods that bordered its bank. He stripped the stallion and was leading it to drink when a jackrabbit popped out of the gloom. The Colt seemed to blossom in his hand. A single shot, and the rabbit lay twitching in spasms.

It was a gamble, firing a gun. Fargo had to pray no Apaches heard, or come morning they would investigate. Holding the rabbit by the ears, he let the Ovaro slake its thirst, then returned to Gwen. After gathering wood, he used his fire steel and flint to start a small fire. The toothpick made short shrift of butchering their supper. Fargo impaled bite-sized chunks on a makeshift spit. Soon the delicious fragrance of roasting meat wafted among the trees.

Fargo was starved enough to eat the rabbit raw. His mouth watered in keen relish as he slowly rotated the meat so it would cook evenly. A groan informed him that his companion was reviving. He gave the spit a few more turns.

"I hate you."

Fargo touched a piece and licked his finger. "You woke up just in time. In another minute or so we can eat."

"Didn't you hear me? I hate you."

"I heard you." Fargo faced around. Gwen was propped on her elbows, glaring at him. "I did what I had to."

"Those soldiers. Burt. All dead. If we had a shred of the same courage they did, we would have died at their side."

"Throwing our lives away isn't my idea of courage."

Gwen sat up and rubbed her jaw. "Easy for you to say. You're the one who ran off and left them."

Fargo was patient with her. "What good would it have done for us to die? What purpose would it serve? I'll tell you. We would have thrown our lives away for nothing. And Melissa and Buck would be on their own."

"So you're saying you ran off to save them? You expect me to believe that?"

"Them, and you. But believe what you want." Fargo devoted himself to their supper. The odor was intoxicating. He pinched off a piece and set it on his tongue to test. The taste nearly made him drool.

Gwen would not let the matter drop. "Did I ask you to save me? No. I told you to leave. But you had to be the hero. Am I right?"

"Whatever you say."

"I hate you," Gwen repeated, and rose. She came to the fire but she deliberately moved to the other side and sank down across from him. Hesitantly, as if afraid the food was a figment of her imagination, she bent low and sniffed several times. "Lordy. It's been so long since I ate last, I bet my stomach has shrunk to the size of a marble."

"He's alive."

Gwen couldn't take her eyes off the meat. "Who is?"

"Raidler. I saw them take him. Tomorrow I'm going after him."

"You're sure? Why would they keep him alive when they slaughtered everyone else?" She blanched. "They're going to torture him, aren't they? How do you know he'll even be alive by morning?"

"I don't. But I'm wore out, you're wore out, and my stallion is on its last legs. We need rest or we won't be of any use to anyone. We'll end up just like those troopers."

Gwen studied him. "Maybe I was a bit harsh. Maybe I misjudged you. But I still feel bad about deserting Burt and those poor cavalrymen."

"Would you feel better if the Apaches had you in their clutches, too? Instead of complaining, you have a lot you should be thankful for." Fargo lifted the spit and blew on the simmering chunks. "But I've learned my lesson. The next time you want to die, I'll let you."

"You're being sarcastic."

"Me? I don't even know what the word means." Fargo peeled off a dripping piece and held it out. "You must be as hungry as I am, so try not to bite my fingers."

Despite herself, Gwen Pearson grinned. Accepting, she sniffed some more, then rimmed her mouth with her pink tongue. "I can't describe how good this smells. Now if only we had some coffee and fresh bread and butter to go with it."

Fargo shook his head. There was no satisfying some people. The ones who, if they stumbled on a vein of gold, would complain because they had to go to the trouble of digging it out of the ground before they could spend it. "Don't wolf your meal or you'll be sick. Take small bites until your stomach grows used to food again."

"Do you think I don't know that? You must believe I'm awful dumb." Gwen bit her piece in half. "Believe it or not,

I learned a lot of things on the farm. I can take care of my-self."

"Lieutenant Jones probably felt the same."

"That was cruel. He gave his life in the service of his country. If I knew how to contact his folks, I'd write them and tell them how well he died. I only hope when my time comes, I die as bravely."

Fargo treated himself to his first bite. His mouth puckered as if he had bitten into a lemon and he had to wait a bit before he could chew. It reminded him of the time he had gone three days without eating on a trek across Death Valley. He had been so famished that when he came on a week-old cougar kill, he had boiled the putrid meat until it was paste and wolfed it down. Somehow, it had stayed down.

"What are you smiling about?"

"Nothing." Fargo did not care to spoil her supper with the revolting details. "When we're done, you turn in and I'll keep first watch."

"Nonsense. Weren't you the one who said Apaches rarely attack at night? Why not sleep? You must be as tired as I am."

"Never take anything for granted," Fargo recited the most important lesson life in the wild had taught him. Anyone who did was either a fool or tired of living.

"I need some more," Gwen said. But rather than reach around the fire, she stood and walked around, taking a seat at his side. "I'll feel like a whole new person before long. All I'd need then to make me as happy as a lark is a bath."

"The stream is that way." Fargo nodded.

Gwen placed a hand on her straggly hair. "Oh, mercy! It's too good to be true." Her eyes narrowed. "But can I trust you to behave like a perfect gentleman?"

"No."

About to take a bite, Gwen laughed. "I admire a man who's honest. Most would lie and sneak up on me in the dark to take a peek, or worse." Her teeth sheared the meat and she talked with her mouth full. "Like Burt said about that Cherokee friend of his, you'd do to ride the river with."

Fargo couldn't let her comment pass. "I thought you hated me?"

"That was five minutes ago. This is now. A gal has the right to change her mind, doesn't she?"

"Now and then," Fargo said, and she didn't catch on that he was being sarcastic again. "But I should warn you. The only blanket we have is the saddle blanket. You'll be cold after you get out of the water."

Gwen snorted. "How delicate do you think I am? I told you, didn't I, that I could beat my brothers at wrestling any day of the week? The oldest, Hiram, outweighed me by seventy or eighty pounds but I pinned him every time. Care to give it a go yourself?"

Fargo imagined grappling with her. "No thanks." No man could concentrate with her ripe, vibrant body pressed against his own. The fondness her brothers had for wrestling took on a whole new meaning. "I'll pass."

"Too bad. It would be fun."

They finished the meal in silence. Fargo set some aside for breakfast, a handful for her and a strip the size of his little finger for himself. Wrapping it all in his extra shirt, he stuffed the shirt back in his saddlebags.

Gwen sat gazing into the fire awhile, deep in thought, then stretched and stood. "Why not?" she said.

"Why not what?" Fargo asked.

"I think I'll take that bath now. If I give a holler, come running." Humming softly, Gwen skipped off.

It wasn't long before Fargo heard splashing and girlish giggling. Making himself comfortable, he broke several branches and stacked them for later use. A multitude of stars sparkled on high. Out in the chaparral coyotes yipped.

"Skye! Skye! Come quick!"

The urgent cry brought Fargo on the run. Colt in hand, he rushed through the dark to the edge of the stream. He saw no one, heard no sounds. Fearful Apaches had abducted her, he crouched and whispered, "Where are you?"

"Right here." A pale shape rose out of a shallow pool.

"Are you all right? What was the shouting about? What do you need me for?"

The shape sashayed closer. "I need someone to scrub my back. Know where I can find a volunteer?"

11

Skye Fargo was angry. With good cause. What Gwen Pearson had done was thoughtless, almost childish. He had been genuinely concerned, afraid she had come to harm. He wasn't the least bit amused.

Yet when the country girl waded up to him, her splendid body shimmering with beads of moisture, as exquisite as the finest sculpture ever rendered, Fargo's anger evaporated. In its place lust was kindled, lust that put a lump in his throat and stirred his manhood. Newfound energy coursed through his limbs, temporarily erasing his fatigue. He slid the Colt into his holster and stood waiting.

"What's the matter?" Gwen teased. "Cat got your tongue?" She gazed up at him with an impish grin. "I really do need someone to wash my back for me."

Fargo's carnal hunger mounted. She was lovely. Although smaller than Melissa Starr and not as amply endowed, Gwen was perfectly proportioned and beautiful in her own right. Her small but firm breasts were naturally upthrust in enticing invitation. Her large nipples were erect with desire. She was tanned from being outdoors so much, and her muscles were finely toned from hard work. A flat stomach flared into nicely curved hips, while water dripped from the pale thatch at the junction of her creamy thighs.

"Something wrong?" Gwen asked when he neither moved nor spoke.

"I can't make up my mind whether to kiss you or spank you."

Gwen giggled. "You're making this hard for me. I thought the man was always supposed to make the first move."

"You want me, do you?" Fargo bluntly asked, still not moving. He was challenging her, taunting her, paying her back for her little prank.

"Damn you." Gwen smiled when she said it. "Is this some sort of game? Do you want me to come right out and admit it? Would that make you happy?"

Fargo did not say a word.

"I hate you more than ever," Gwen declared. Then she stepped even closer and craned her neck so she could kiss him warmly on the chin, on the cheek, on the edge of his mouth. Her breath was warm, her touch velvet. "Yes, I want you," she said hungrily. "I think I've wanted you since the moment I laid eyes on you. But I'm not the kind of woman who throws herself at a man. It's taken me a while to build up the nerve."

"Why here? Why now?"

"I thought of waiting until we got to Tucson, but then I remembered you're going east, not west. This might be my last chance. Ever." Gwen's throat bobbed. "I'm scared the Apaches will catch us. Scared I'll never get to touch you or any other man ever again, never get to—"

Fargo silenced her by pressing his mouth to hers. She responded by melting into his arms, her small figure fitting snugly against him as if their two bodies were but two parts of a whole. Her lips were downy soft yet firm with passion. Almost timidly, they parted to allow his tongue to gain entrance. Her tongue was small, delicate, yet silken. It met his, exploring, then entwined in an erotic dance.

Fargo's hands rose up the backs of her thighs. Her legs trembled as he ran his fingertips to her firm buttocks and cupped them, feeling the heat she radiated. She mewed deep in her throat as he kneaded her. Then he slid his hands higher, his palms rubbing across her lower back, rising on either side of her curved spine to her shoulders. She was still wet, her skin wonderfully cool. Fargo massaged her shoulders, then ran a hand through her damp hair.

Gwen broke to take a breath. "Ohhhhh, I'm in heaven."

"You're not halfway there yet," Fargo said, and kissed her brow, her cheeks, her ear. She was sensitive there, and when his tongue flicked her earlobe, she gasped and arched against him. He sucked on it, feeling her quiver, her legs rubbing against one another to heighten her pleasure.

Fargo pulled back. He removed his hat, peeled off his dirty shirt, his gunbelt, his pants, and his boots. That tiny voice at the back of his mind came to life. It railed at him for letting down his guard in the middle of Apache country. "You're being stupid!" the voice screamed. Fargo didn't care. The past two days had been a living hell. He would like a short time to relax, to forget the problems he faced.

Gwen stared at him as she might at a steak she was about to devour. "You're magnificent," she husked, her small hands rising to his superbly muscled chest. Her palms rubbed in tiny circles, working their way to his broad shoulders, then down his arms. She drank in the sight of him, breathing heavier and heavier.

Fargo elicited a sharp gasp by suddenly cupping her breasts. They fit his hands like large apples, the nipples full and taut. He gently squeezed, then with more force. Gwen gazed skyward, her rosy lips parted as if to cry out, but she uttered no sound other than panting. Fargo stroked her, from the base of her cones outward. He pulled on her nipples and tweaked them, and she groaned so long and loud that he started to worry about the Apaches again.

To quiet her, Fargo smothered her mouth with his own. Her kiss this time was fiery hot, her tongue a dervish that never stopped encircling his. He continued to grope her mounds and pinch her nipples until her chest heaved with passion.

"Please," Gwen said. "Please, please, please."

Fargo did not know exactly what she wanted. Bending, he

clamped his lips onto a pert breast and inhaled it. She rose onto her toes, her nails raking his shoulders.

"Like that, like that!"

Her breasts swelled under his manipulating fingers. Fargo lathered them with his tongue, then licked lower to her navel. The musky scent that rose from her nether region tingled his nostrils. He slowly straightened, kissing her belly, kissing between her breasts, her lower neck, her mouth. She glued herself to him, her hips pumping.

Fargo shocked her by taking her hand and placing it on his pole. At the contact, Gwen stiffened, then began to stroke him from top to bottom. Relaxing, she drew back to admire his manliness, and for a few seconds Fargo thought she might dip lower but she didn't. Closing his eyes, he thrilled to her tender touch. Then he opened them, clasped her, and plunged his right hand between her legs.

Gwen cried out. As well she might. Fargo's fingers were enveloped in moist heat that became hotter the deeper he went. His index finger found her slick tunnel and he thrust it in to the knuckle.

"Ohhhhh! Skye!"

Her bottom heaved as Fargo pumped in and out, the friction adding to the already considerable heat, to say nothing of her pleasure. Gwen bit his shoulder. Her greedy mouth rose to his and fused. She cooed like a dove as he brought her to the brink of release, but only to the brink. Her hips were rising up and down, her legs shaking uncontrollably, when he stopped stroking and placed both hands on her hips.

"What—?" Gwen said.

Fargo lifted her off the ground. Her small frame, her light weight, made it easy. Easy, too, to poise her over his manhood. She understood and willingly parted her legs. Then, inch by iron inch, Fargo slid her down onto himself, inserting his pole into her wet sheath. He took her standing up, his sturdy legs bracing them both. And when he was in her all the way, when she was balanced on his hips, he gripped her shoulders and thrust higher, rising onto the tips of his toes.

"Ahhhhh! Yessssss!"

Gwen threw back her head, her eyelids fluttering, golden tresses spilling over her shoulders. She gave herself up to him completely, adrift in the ecstasy of their coupling, crying "Oh! Oh! Oh!" each time he hammered into her.

Fargo pumped and pumped, in perfect self-control, staving off his release for as long as he wanted. Gwen thrashed and writhed, her hands on his powerful arms, her tiny feet barely touching the ground.

While their union lasted, for those precious moments in time, the sensations they felt overwhelmed their worries, their cares. The Apaches were shut from their minds, the sense of constant danger temporarily gone. Their release was just as much mental and emotional as it was physical, which added to the intensity of their mutual climax.

Gwen wailed like a lost soul as her body was flooded by rapture. She clung to his shoulders, her hips levering wildly, her womanhood wrapped around his member like a glove. And when she called out, when she said, "Oh, Skye! I'm coming again!" it triggered his own release.

Fargo exploded with the force of a keg of black powder, ramming up into her again and again and again. To call what he felt bliss did not do it justice. He crested a white hot peak and sailed on the inner winds of blinding pleasure.

When, at long, long last, Fargo slowed and then stopped, they were both spent, both slick with sweat, both breathing as if they could not catch their breath. Fargo held on to her and sagged onto the bank, stones and dirt prickling his skin. Gwen's hands were on his neck, her lips on his chest.

"I thought I would die."

Fargo listened to the night sounds, his wariness returning. Coyotes were in full chorus, and to the west an owl hooted. Much farther off a panther screeched. All was normal. All was well. He sighed and ran a hand over her hair. "Thank you."

Gwen tittered.

"Share the joke," Fargo said.

"I guess I don't hate you anymore."

"Really? You could have fooled me."

Both of them smiled and closed their eyes, and although Fargo did not want to fall asleep just yet, he dozed, awakening half an hour later with Gwen snoring lightly on top of him. Water chilled his feet. The cool night air caressed their bodies. He started to sit up, and Gwen lifted her head. Befuddled by sleep, she looked all around.

"What is it? The Apaches? Have they found us?"

Fargo kissed her cheek. "No. It's peaceful as can be." He rose, cradling her. "I need to wash up and get dressed."

"We'll wash together."

They stepped into the shallow pool and sat facing one another. The water was only five or six inches deep, the pool no wider than four or five feet, but it was so cool, so refreshing. Fargo splashed his legs, his chest, then cupped his hands and drenched his face and hair. He would have liked to sit there until morning, luxuriating in the coolness.

Gwen washed her arms, her face. Leaning back, she quirked her lips and said, "This is a no-no time I'll never forget."

"A what?" Fargo asked.

"A no-no. When I was growing up, whenever I was bad my ma would say I had done a no-no. It was no-no this, and no-no that. Taking a cookie without permission, leaving my room a mess, that sort of thing. It got so I learned to be real secretive about the no-no things I did. I'd never tell a soul." Gwen bent a shapely leg and idly ran a finger along her inner thigh. "This is a no-no time I'll treasure forever."

Fargo was watching her finger, how it slowly swirled around and around. He saw her glistening thatch and the water flowing between her thighs, and he began to grow hard again.

"Was I all right for you?" Gwen asked. "As you've probably guessed, I don't have a lot of experience. You're only the second man I've ever made love to."

Fargo grew harder.

"I was ashamed the last time. It was a boy I knew, one I always figured I'd marry. But I'm not ashamed with you. Why should that be?" Gwen looked down at herself. "I know I'm not the most beautiful woman in the world. I'm too small up top, for one thing." She cupped her breasts. "If you only knew—"

But Fargo didn't care to hear more. He surged toward her, enfolded her in his arms, and parted her legs with his knees.

Gwen's eyes went wide. "Again? So soon?"

His answer was to drive into her, nearly lifting her out of the water with the urgency of his thrust. There was no kissing this time, no foreplay. Holding her slender waist, Fargo lanced up into her, over and over and over. She bent her head back and groaned nonstop, adrift in a sensual sea of delight.

Fargo lasted longer this time. Much, much longer. A riptide of arousal pulled him higher and higher until he was at the summit with nowhere to go but over the brink. He prolonged the inevitable as long as he could, extending their bliss for what seemed like forever. At last the eruption came, so violent, so intense, the stars pranced giddily and the ground seemed to buck as if from an earthquake. Gwen sank her teeth into his shoulder to stifle a shriek.

Tired but fulfilled, they leaned against each other, Fargo stroking her hair. Gwen looked up at him in awe and asked, "Don't you ever get enough?"

Fargo knew women well. He gave her a compliment she would treasure. "It's you. You do things to a man."

"I do?" Gwen said in disbelief. "Why hasn't anyone ever told me before? You'd think I'd have men falling out of the trees to ask me out."

Shrugging, Fargo replied, "You know how men are. We like to keep our feelings to ourselves. And most men get tongue-tied around a pretty woman."

"Land o' Goshen! I sure am learning a lot tonight. Anything else you have a hankering to teach me?" Gwen wriggled her bottom.

Fargo laughed and smacked her on the fanny. "And you

think I never get enough? On your feet, hussy. We need sleep now, more than anything else."

"Speak for yourself," Gwen groused.

Glowing embers were all that remained of the fire. Fargo rekindled it and stretched out. Gwen snuggled against him, her cheek on his chest, her fingers playing with his beard. She did not fall asleep right away. On the verge of dozing off, he heard her clear her throat.

"Skye?"

"Mmm?"

"I—" Gwen hesitated, giving Fargo a suspicion of what was to come. "I take it you're not looking to settle down any time soon?"

"No."

"Then I guess you wouldn't want—"

"No."

"Oh." Gwen slid off him and rested her head in her arms. "I hate you again."

"Good." Chuckling, Fargo rolled onto his side and was soon dreaming of Denver and clean sheets and the best whiskey to be had. A poke in the ribs woke him up. Gwen had turned in her sleep so her back was against him, and she mumbled something about needing to milk the cows. Fargo drifted off once more.

Shortly before dawn a splash in the stream snapped Fargo awake. His hand closed on the Henry, but it was only a deer, a doe, come for her morning drink. Shaking himself to get his blood flowing, Fargo rose. To heat the leftover rabbit, he ignited kindling and added fuel.

Along about the time the meat was ready, Gwen rose on an elbow and dreamily watched him. "Morning."

"We head out in ten minutes."

"Fine." Like a contented cat, Gwen lazily arched her spine and sat up. "I still feel as if I'm floating on a cloud. Never knew a man could have this effect on me."

"I thought you were back to hating me?"

Gwen ruffled her hair and smacked her lips. "I'll hate you later. Right now I'm in too good a mood."

Truth to tell, so was Fargo. But that changed once they were in the saddle and trotting to the southeast. He had to shut the pleasure they had shared from his mind. The Apaches were still abroad and they must occupy him now. They, and they alone.

Over an hour passed. The grass shimmered in the morning sun. Sparrows flitted on the breeze. A herd of antelope sped away at dazzling speed.

Fargo planned to reach the road somewhere near the stand of oaks, but his sense of direction was so exact that he came out of the grass directly across from it. No sounds issued from within the stand, nor were any living creatures to be seen. No birds, no squirrels, nothing.

"It's so quiet," Gwen said. "You don't suppose something awful happened?"

"We'll find out." Fargo crossed the road and passed between two trunks. Suddenly a pistol cracked, the slug thumping into the bole on the left. Fargo reined to the right, where the oaks were thicker, and produced the Colt. But a female voice, raised in anger, froze his finger on the trigger.

"Tucker, you damned idiot! Didn't you see who that is?" Melissa Starr was fit to be tied. "Skye? Did he hit you? It's safe to come out in the open."

The redhead and the drummer were at the edge of the clearing. Melissa was radiant, as always. Virgil Tucker sheepishly held a smoking revolver.

Beyond them, propped against a log, was Buck Dawson, chewing on a wad of tobacco. "Fargo! Miss Pearson!" the driver hailed them. "Don't pay that yack Tucker any mind! He's so scared, it's a wonder he ain't shot his own foot off."

Gwen hopped down, saying, "It's so good to see all of you alive." She embraced each of them, even the drummer. "We have so much to tell you! Don't we, Skye?" Gwen glanced up at him. "Aren't you stepping down?"

"No," Fargo responded. He had a lot to do and little time

in which to do it. "You're to stay here until I get back."
Fargo noticed that the color had returned to Buck Dawson's
cheeks, that Melissa had ripped more strips from her dress
and changed the bandages on Buck's wound, and that Virgil
Tucker was even more of a mess than when Fargo saw him
last. Tucker's clothes were filthy, his jacket torn, his shoes
so scuffed it would take a month of polishing to restore
them. Fargo also noticed that something was missing, something important. "Where are the horses?"

Melissa and Dawson looked at Tucker. "Well?" the redhead said.

The drummer gestured. "I'm sorry, Fargo. I lost them."

Fargo couldn't believe what he was hearing. "How in the
hell can you lose an entire team?"

"It's not my fault. I was on my way back, just like you
told me. I had to heed Nature's call, so I stopped and went
into some bushes. When I came out they were running off. I
tried to catch them. Honestly I did. But they wouldn't stop."

Fargo gripped the saddle horn to keep from climbing
down and gripping Tucker by the throat. "Did you tie them
to anything? A tree? A bush?"

"No."

"Did you hobble some, at least?"

"It never occurred to me."

"You just got down and walked away and left them standing there?" Fargo had heard of some stupid stunts in his
time, but this! And drummers were supposed to be so
shrewd! They had to be, in order to manipulate others into
buying their wares.

Virgil Tucker glumly nodded. "I just wasn't thinking, I
guess."

"Of all the—" Fargo stopped before he vented his spleen.
Without the horses it would be doubly hard to elude the
Apaches. Instead of half a day's ride, it would take close to
two days to reach the San Simon, Buck Dawson's leg hurt
like it was. "Where did you lose them?"

"Where?"

"Are you hard of hearing? Exactly where did they run off? Once I've found Burt Raidler, I'll track them down."

"I don't recall, exactly," Tucker said. "Somewhere between where I saw you last and here."

"That's a big help." Fargo thought of another way to pinpoint where he should start tracking "How long after we parted company did it happen? Fifteen minutes? An hour? What?"

Tucker scratched the stubble dotting his double chin. "Again, I'm sorry. I wasn't paying much attention. I really can't say."

A strong urge to punch the drummer came over Fargo, but he resisted. It struck him as peculiar that Tucker couldn't remember a single thing. Any man able to memorize profit margins on dozens of products had to have a better-than-average memory.

Melissa was as peeved as Fargo. "You never said anything about losing the team when you straggled in here, Virgil. When were you fixing to tell us? Next Fourth of July?"

"It just never came up, is all," Tucker said.

"Who are you trying to kid?" Melissa jabbed him. "You knew Buck and I would be mad so you kept quiet to save yourself a tongue-lashing."

Tucker stared at the ground. "I can't put anything past you, can I? But I felt so miserable. I knew how much those animals meant to us." He glanced up, pleading, "Can you find it in your hearts to forgive me? It's not as if I lost the horses on purpose. I just don't ride very often. I'm a salesman, not a frontiersman."

Melissa's anger faded. "Since you asked so sweetly, I won't hold it against you."

"Me, neither," Buck Dawson said. "Some folks can't help being as dumb as a shovel. It's in their blood, I reckon."

Fargo wasn't feeling as charitable. He was convinced Tucker was lying, even though he had to admit it made no sense. What did the man hope to gain? "How are you fixed for food, Melissa?"

"We have over half the pemmican left. Buck and I have been rationing it, a few pieces a couple of times a day." The redhead patted her stomach. "I'm half starved, but I'll be ten pounds thinner when I make my debut in San Francisco."

Dawson spat tobacco juice. "Only a female," he said, and chortled.

Fargo raised the reins. "I can't say when I'll be back. If I'm not here by tomorrow morning, don't wait for me. Head east. Travel at night. Make Buck a crutch so he can keep up." He wheeled the pinto to leave but Gwen Pearson stepped in close to him and placed a hand on his leg. Melissa, a second later, did the same on the other side.

"Don't let those devils get their hands on you, Skye," Gwen said. At that exact moment, Melissa declared, "Keep your hair on, handsome."

The two women stopped talking. Their eyes met over the saddle's pommel. Resentment gave way to growing shock.

"No!" Melissa said.

"It can't be!" Gwen replied.

"You, too?"

"Surely he didn't!"

"Both of us?"

"I'll be switched!"

Fargo touched his hat brim and got out of there before they pulled him from the saddle and stomped him to death. Buck Dawson's rowdy mirth drifted on his heels until he was almost out of the stand. He looked back and saw both women glaring at him with their hands on their hips.

There was a lot for Fargo to ponder as he rode westward. Unless he learned where Chipota's band was holed up, Texas would soon be one cowpuncher poorer. It was unlikely they were still at the basin. They'd want a new site, safe from discovery. And near water.

Three-quarters of an hour later Fargo abruptly reined up. A line of tracks crossed the road, tracks made by horses traveling from south to north in single file. Tracks made two mornings ago.

"Tucker, you lying son of a bitch." Fargo understood now why the drummer had pretended to be so forgetful. Vowing to settle accounts if the Apaches didn't put windows in his skull, Fargo trotted on in search of the most ruthless renegade in Arizona history.

12

Chipota's new camp was in a narrow canyon with only one way in or out, a game trail worn by deer and sundry creatures that came to drink at a spring situated deep in the canyon's depths. It was a natural fortress, and here a small force could hold off an army, if need be. By posting warriors near the entrance, the wily Apache leader had insured that his enemies couldn't approach undetected.

But what Chipota did not count on was that a resourceful rider might find a way to the *top* of the canyon. It was a hard climb and would daunt most. Yet if a man were skilled enough, as Skye Fargo was, and his mount were surefooted enough, as the Ovaro was, it could be done.

Skye Fargo had been on his belly for over an hour, spying on the band. He saw warriors come and go, saw a mule being butchered for their evening meal, saw Chipota in council. He also spotted Burt Raidler and another captive staked out near the spring. Both men had been stripped to the waist. Neither moved the whole time Fargo watched, and he feared the Texan was dead.

It had taken Fargo most of the day to track the band to their new lair. In half an hour the sun would set. He must be in position by then, so he slid back from the edge, rose, and mounted. Descending took almost the entire thirty minutes. After secreting the Ovaro, he proceeded on foot to the trail leading into the canyon. When he was an arrow's flight from the entrance, he sank onto his belly again.

Now came the part no sane man would attempt.

An Apache was positioned on either side of the trail near the canyon's mouth. Both were hidden in rocks, safe from prying eyes. Except from above. Fargo knew exactly where they were. He knew that each was some twenty feet from the opening, and slightly above it. He also knew that once it was dark, they wouldn't be able to see much of the trail although the slightest sound would arouse their suspicion.

Fargo was going to attempt what no one had ever attempted before. He was going to sneak *into* an Apache stronghold right under the noses of their sentries. To succeed, he must not make the slightest noise. One mistake, and he would pay for his folly with his life.

The shadows lengthened. Gradually the sky darkened. Sparkling stars appeared. By then it was pitch black on the canyon floor, so dark than when Fargo extended an arm, he couldn't see his hand. He was ready.

Apaches had keen eyesight but even they had limits. They weren't the inhuman devils most whites made them out to be. They were flesh and blood, no more, no less.

Fargo counted on the sentries staying where they were once night fell. If they didn't, if they had moved closer to the trail, he would never make it into the canyon. Sliding out from behind a boulder, he crawled toward the opening. He moved one limb at a time, ever so slowly, ever so carefully. Every few feet he stopped to listen.

The trail was no more than three feet wide, more often less. It wound like a serpent, which worked in Fargo's favor. Except for the final thirty feet. That was where he would be in the most danger.

Fargo was almost to the straight stretch when something he had hoped wouldn't happen, happened. He heard the light tread of someone coming up behind him. Small boulders to his right offered the only haven. He slid in among them, flattening and removing his hat as shapes materialized in the night, moving rapidly. His cheek pressed flat, Fargo saw a stocky warrior go by, then another and another. Eight warriors, returning late without spoils or additional captives.

One of the sentries called out and was answered by one of the newcomers. The eight stopped and made small talk. The name Shis-Inday was used, which was how the Apaches referred to themselves, "The People of the Woods" was the rough translation. Fargo also heard the Apache word for "soldiers," something about a patrol, but he could not quite catch what was being said. Presently, the warriors hastened into their stronghold.

Fargo lay where he was for the longest time. The sentries would be more alert for a while. He must let them settle down. When he deemed it safe, he snaked to the trail and went on. The short hairs at the nape of his neck prickled as he crawled around the last bend onto the straight stretch. Ten yards of no cover. Ten yards where the scrape of an elbow or knee or a dislodged stone could cost his life.

Every nerve jangling, Fargo slunk forward, all his movements in slow motion. They had to be, for any sharp motion was bound to draw attention. He would slide his left arm, then his right, then rise slightly on his elbows and propel himself by his knees so his stomach wouldn't brush the ground.

Fargo was directly between the sentries when the one on the right suddenly stood up. Fargo turned to stone. The warrior was staring off down the trail, but at what Fargo had no idea. Afraid more warriors were returning, he was anxious to hide but he couldn't move without the sentry being aware.

Seconds became a minute. Two. Fargo scarcely breathed. He glanced out the corner of his other eye but did not see the other sentry. After an eternity the first man sank below the rocks.

Fargo did not waste another second crawling into the canyon. Several hundred yards from end to end, it broadened into an irregular oval. The Apaches were gathered in the center, most clustered around a fire. The mules that had not yet been eaten were tied close to the right-hand cliff. So were the horses from the stage, the team that had been in Virgil Tucker's care.

Rising, Fargo crept to the left. A thin belt of vegetation, mostly high weeds with a few shrub trees, provided the cover he needed to reach the captives. But again he had to move with painstaking slowness. Whenever a warrior's gaze roved in his general direction, he stopped. It helped that the Apaches were at ease, relaxing in the safety of their sanctuary. Chipota came to the fire and hunkered.

Once past them Fargo moved faster. Parting a clump of grass, he saw the two spread-eagle figures. Burt Raidler's chest rose up and down, so the cowboy wasn't dead, after all. The other man showed no evidence of life even up close. From the rim Fargo had recognized who it was, and it had come as no surprise.

A glance verified none of the Apaches were nearby. Fargo crawled to the Texan, whose face was puffy and discolored, his lips split. Raidler also had a shallow cut in his side. The Apaches had treated him roughly but hadn't tortured him. Yet.

Fargo placed a hand over the cowboy's mouth, then shook him. Nothing happened. Fargo did it again, eliciting a groan. He clamped his hand tighter to muffle the sound and stared at the war party, whose only interest was a roasting haunch.

"Burt," Fargo whispered. "Can you hear me?"

Raidler groaned again, more softly. His eyelids opened, closed, opened again. Dulled by pain, they betrayed confusion. He tried to speak.

"Chipota's bunch caught you," Fargo quickly whispered. "I'm here to get you out. If you understand, nod once."

The Texan nodded.

Fargo removed his hand. "I'll cut you loose in a minute," he said. "How's the leg? Do you think you can ride?"

Raidler had to swallow a few times before he could reply. "I don't have much choice, do I, pard? It's either ride or die." He paused. "You're plumb loco, comin' after me. I'm grateful, mind you, but I don't want you to die on my account. Just cut me loose and sneak on out. I'll wait a spell, then try to get away on my own."

"Nothing doing," Fargo whispered. In the shape Raidler was in, he'd never make it to the canyon mouth. "Lie still. I'll be right back."

Twisting, Fargo moved to the other captive. William Frazier III had been dead quite a while. A knife thrust between the ribs was to blame. But he hadn't been mutilated, a sign he had met his end bravely. His face was set in a sad expression tinged with regret. Both eyes were wide open, fixed on the firmament. Fargo closed them, then drew the Arkansas toothpick.

Burt Raidler was watching the Apaches. "Hurry, pard," he said as Fargo began cutting. "I reckon those varmints will be back to finish me off any minute now."

"Not until after they've eaten," Fargo guessed. "We have time yet."

"Do we? There's one comin' toward us now."

Fargo looked. A Chiricahua was walking toward the end of the canyon, a Sharps cradled in his brawny arms. "Don't move." Sliding into the shadows, Fargo rested a hand on the Colt. If the Apaches discovered him, he'd never make it out of the canyon alive. There were too many of them. They'd bottle up the entrance, light torches, and search him out. Unless he could flap his arms and fly, his days of roaming the mountains and plains would be over.

But the warrior with the Sharps wasn't interested in the captives. He went to the spring for a drink, then strolled back to the fire without displaying any interest in Raidler and Frazier.

Fargo snuck to the Texan. "Are you strong enough to stand?"

"I'm as weak as pond water. But if you need me to, I will." Raidler started to rise.

"Not yet. When you hear me yell, get up. Once I have you on a horse, stay low. Leave the rest to me."

Raidler was going to say something but Fargo gestured for him to keep quiet, pivoted, and padded toward the animals. The mules and horses were on separate strings, the horses nearer the high cliff. Fargo freed them first, working swiftly, patting each and speaking softly so none would wander off before he was ready. Next, he cut the mules loose. Then, grasping the mane of a sorrel, he swung up. His Colt took the place of the Arkansas toothpick.

Fargo had planned to wait until the warriors were eating but another Apache rose and came toward the spring. Straightening, Fargo gave voice to a piercing war whoop that would do any Sioux proud. The lusty, bloodcurdling cry ran out loud and strident. Simultaneously, Fargo banged off a shot at the Apache bound for the spring. As the man toppled, the mules and the horses whirled and stampeded off up the canyon—toward the startled Apaches.

Confusion reigned. Fargo, pulling on the rope to a spare horse, flew to the captives. Burt Raidler was trying to rise. But hampered by his broken leg, he could not quite manage it. Fargo vaulted off the sorrel, wrapped an arm around the Texan's midsection, and literally threw the cowboy onto the bay. "Hang on!"

The stampeding mules and horses were almost to the center. Bunched together, they thundered down on the warriors, who scattered, running every which way. A couple were too slow and paid for their sloth by being battered aside. One was trampled, his shrieks when a leg was shattered adding to the mayhem.

Gripping the bay's rope, Fargo galloped toward the canyon mouth. He stayed in the shadows, close to the cliff. The Apaches were in a state of total confusion, milling about, some waving their arms to try and stop the animals. He was almost abreast of the fire when a swarthy shape hove up out of the murk. The warrior saw him and went for a pistol tucked under a belt. Fargo's Colt boomed once.

At the shot, Apaches everywhere turned. Those on the other side of the canyon could not see Fargo but those on the near side could, and howls of rage pealed off the high walls as they sped to head him off.

Fargo had to shoot another one. Then he was past the fire,

past most of the renegades. The fleetest were in determined pursuit. Rapidly outdistancing them, Fargo saw the welcome sight of the entrance ahead. Not so welcome was the appearance of the two sentries, who had rushed in to see what the uproar was about.

The fleeing horses and mules barreled into the gap. The two sentries scampered for their lives, one high into the rocks, the other pressing against the wall. After the last of the animals had gone by, he sprang to bar the sorrel from following suit.

Fargo shot the man down, then twisted and snapped another shot at the sentry in the rocks, who was raising a rifle. The warrior clutched at his chest, tottered, and fell. Another few moments and Fargo was out of the canyon. Guns cracked, lead sizzling the air. Fully half the band had given chase.

Raidler was still atop the bay, clinging desperately to its mane, his face as white as that of a ghostly specter.

Fargo raced to the spot where he had to branch off from the trail. He was well ahead of the Apaches, but his lead was not so great that he could afford to be careless. Going a short distance, he reined up so they wouldn't hear him, and waited. He did not wait long.

Warriors streamed off along the game trail. The racket made by the fleeing animals lured them on. They assumed Fargo was ahead of them. Presently, the sounds of padding feet and jumbled voices faded, so Fargo kneed the sorrel on to the gulch where he had hid the Ovaro.

The Texan marshaled a wan grin. "We did it, pard! We skunked those hombres!"

"Yell a little louder, why don't you?"

After switching to the stallion, Fargo reloaded the Colt, flipped the loading gate closed, and took hold of the ropes to the bay and the sorrel. Although the stand of oaks was to the east, he headed due west. With the countryside swarming with angry Apaches, he'd decided to take a roundabout route back. It would take longer but be safer.

Fargo rode slowly, frequently stopping to probe the darkness. After a couple of hours went by without a hitch, he congratulated himself on eluding the war party.

But he did so too soon.

They had turned to the north to work their way to the gorge. Raidler kept flitting in and out of consciousness, sometimes mumbling incoherently. He needed rest, food, and most of all, doctoring.

Fargo was thinking that maybe it would be best to stop and let the cowboy sleep until dawn when the Ovaro pricked its ears and nickered. Halting, he listened, but he heard nothing out of the ordinary, even though they were in open country and noise carried far.

Raidler began to mumble again. Quickly dismounting, Fargo placed a hand over the Texan's mouth. He scoured the desert shrub but did not see anything. When the cowboy quieted down, Fargo led the horses on foot.

The night seemed peaceful enough. All was quiet, the wind included. A multitude of stars bathed the arid terrain in their ethereal glow.

Fargo saw no reason for concern, yet his instincts blared a warning that all was not as it appeared. Something was wrong, something was out of place, but for the life of him he could not figure out what it was.

Out of habit, Fargo drew the Colt. To his left appeared some saguaros, to his right random boulders. Either might conceal Apaches. Since the boulders were the more likely spot, he watched them intently, glancing at the saguaros every so often. It was when he did so for the fourth or fifth time that his instincts proved once again why they should be trusted.

One of the saguaros had *moved*. The saguaro was a cactus plant with a thick trunk and upturned arms that gave it a vaguely human aspect. And one of the lower arms on one of the saguaros had changed position.

Fargo stopped but did not let on that he knew. Walking to the bay, he pretended to examine Raidler. He was buying time to think. The Apaches wouldn't spring their ambush until he was a little closer, or if he tried to get away. But that was out of the question. With Raidler passed out, the cowboy couldn't stay on his mount. He'd fall and be slain.

Since Fargo couldn't watch over the Texan and fight off the Apaches both, he must do what the Apaches least expected. The Texan mumbled again. Fargo, sliding the revolver into its holster, bent over as if listening to the gibberish. When Raidler fell silent, he stepped to the Ovaro and reached out as if to grip the reins. But his hand closed on the Henry's stock instead. The rifle was in his hands before the Apaches could suspect what he was up to. Levering a round into the chamber, he fired at the trunk of the saguaro that had seemed to move.

Two of the cactus's arms flapped like the wings of an ungainly bird as the warrior crouched behind it was flung to the ground.

A command was barked and the rest broke from cover, three from the boulders, two more from the saguaros. Several had guns and they were the ones Fargo dropped first, firing as fast as he could work the Henry. Then the remaining two were on him, one wielding a lance, the other a war club.

The latter was Chipota.

A swing of the lance brought it crashing down on the rifle's barrel. Fargo held on and spun to shoot but the war club caught him across the right forearm, a grazing blow that numbed him from the elbow to the tips of his fingers. He backpedaled to gain room to move but another sweep of the long lance jarred the Henry from his grasp.

Chipota growled a few words at the other warrior, then came in low while the other one came in high.

Fargo couldn't draw the Colt because his right hand was next to useless. His fingers tingled madly and wouldn't clench tight enough to grip the butt. He avoided a lance thrust, a flash of the club. The Apaches were so eager to finish him off that in their rush to get at him, they crowded one another.

Fargo skipped backward, away from the horses, away from the helpless Texan. When the Apache holding the lance glanced at Raidler, Fargo bent, scooped up a handful of dirt, and threw it in the man's face. It drew the warrior's attention but also permitted Chipota to connect again, this time with a searing smash to the thigh that nearly dropped Fargo in his tracks.

The tingling in Fargo's arm was swiftly fading. He could move his fingers but couldn't make a play for the Colt yet. Another thrust of the lance missed by a whisker. With his left hand he grabbed the shaft. The warrior grunted and pulled but couldn't wrest it loose.

Suddenly Chipota swiped viciously at Fargo's hand with his war club. At the last instant Fargo jerked it away and the heavy stone head struck the lance. A resounding *crack,* and the lance was broken, shorter now by a good two feet.

That didn't stop the warrior who held it. The metal tip was gone but the end was tapered to a wicked point. Powered by sufficient force, it could be just as deadly. The Apache lunged, pressing Fargo mercilessly, while Chipota slanted to the left to come at him from a new angle. They were working in concert, the one to occupy him while the other finished him off. A flick of the lance drove Fargo toward the war club. He dodged, spun, and had to sidestep another lethal thrust. The pair were unrelenting, never giving him a second to catch his breath.

Fargo took another step back, and another. The feel of a rock under his heel gave him an idea. Deliberately stumbling, he let his momentum carry him onto his back. He flipped onto his side as the lance sought his heart. Then he rolled, but not away from the warrior, toward him, into the Apache's legs. Whipping his arm around them, Fargo heaved, causing the warrior to totter against Chipota.

It gained Fargo a few precious seconds and he used them to reach across his hip and draw the Colt with his left hand. He was slower than he would normally be but fast enough to level the revolver and thumb back the hammer before the

Apaches recovered. The man armed with the lance raised it and sprang, hatred animating his face.

Fargo fired, the slug slamming the warrior partway around. Other men would have crumbled, but the Apache reputation for toughness was well-earned. The warrior braced himself and hiked the lance to throw it. A second shot catapulted him rearward.

That left Chipota boiling with fury. Raining the war club in a fierce deluge, he tried to bash in Fargo's skull.

Fargo skittered from side to side, like a crab. The club passed so close to his cheek, he felt a gust from its passage. Abruptly, Chipota's barrel chest blotted out the sky. Fargo fired once but Chipota barely slowed, fired a second time, and the leader faltered, firing a third time as Chipota elevated the club. The scourge of the territory tottered, hissing like a serpent.

One shot was left in the Colt. Fargo had to make it count. Firing from the hip, he cored Chipota's skull, but the Chiricahua firebrand was as tenacious as a wolverine. Dead on his feet, he somehow took one more step, then folded. Fargo had to scramble to keep from having the body fall on him.

In the silence that ensued, Fargo retrieved the Henry. The feeling in his right arm had almost been restored. He moved to the bay and stood waiting for more Apaches to appear, but none did. Evidently the band had broken up into small parties and fanned out across the wasteland. Purely by chance, Chipota's bunch had been the one that had spotted him.

Burt Raidler raised partway up. "Pard? Why have we stopped? Are we there yet?"

"No, but we will be by first light."

And Fargo was true to his word. Long hours of wary winding along inky gulches and around benighted hills, through thick brush and across baked flatlands, brought them within sight of the stand of oaks just as pink tinged the eastern rim of the world. Fargo's legs were as heavy as iron, every muscle in his body sore. He guided the plodding Ovaro into the trees.

Buck Dawson was awake, tending a small fire. Beaming, he rose stiffly and shuffled over to greet Fargo and help lower the Texan. The commotion awakened Melissa, Gwen, and Virgil Tucker, who sat up rubbing his eyes. The drummer had been using his folded jacket for a pillow. Now he carefully unfolded it and slipped it on.

"You made it!" Gwen exclaimed happily.

"I knew you would!" Melissa said. "The worst is over!"

Dawson was taking a bite of tobacco. "Ain't you forgettin' that Frazier gent? He's still not accounted for."

"Yes, he is," Fargo revealed. "The Apaches got him."

Gwen sadly sighed. "Another one. But I don't feel as upset about him as I did about that sweet boy, Tommy, and those other fellers. Frazier got what he deserved for killing Mr. Hackman."

Fargo turned to the drummer. "Tell them," he said.

Virgil Tucker acted surprised. "Tell them what?"

"That it wasn't Frazier. It was you."

"You must have been in the sun too long, friend. I haven't the foggiest notion what you're talking about."

Fargo was in no mood to be played for a fool. "You're a lying bastard, Tucker. I found where you crossed the road with the team when you went hunting for Hackman."

Tucker slowly stood. "I told you. They ran off on me."

"No, they weren't bunched up as they would have been if they were on their own. They were being led, in single file." It was why Fargo had been so mad when he found the tracks. He knew the drummer had lied. "You lost the team near where you killed Hackman. Probably the shot spooked them and they ran off. Later, the Apaches found them."

"This is ridiculous." Tucker was sweating despite the morning chill. "Why would I do such a thing?"

"For whatever Hackman had in his valise. Whatever was so valuable, he wouldn't let it out of his sight."

The drummer appealed to the others. "Honestly, none of you believe these wild allegations, do you?" Their cold stares showed they did. Tucker nervously licked his lips.

Then his hand moved, and in it materialized a derringer. "Damn you, Fargo! Why couldn't you leave well enough alone? Now I can't let any of you live."

Gwen Pearson asked the question on all their minds. "In heaven's name, Virgil, what did you hope to gain?"

Tucker pulled a leather wallet from an inner pocket. "Half a million dollars worth of negotiable certificates! Is that reason enough for you?" He cackled at his good fortune. "Elias Hackman wasn't an ordinary stockbroker. He was a courier, taking these stocks to a client in San Francisco. I found out by accident at one of the way stations, when he was writing a letter to his firm and I peeked over his shoulder. Now they're mine!"

Melissa took a step and he pivoted toward her. "Would you really murder all of us, Virgil? I thought we were your friends."

"Lady, for half a million dollars I'd kill my own mother! No more endless days on the go! No more bouncing around in cramped stages! No more sleeping in hovels! From now on, it's only the best for Virgil W. Tucker."

Fargo saw one of the others draw a pistol. He moved, and the drummer swung toward him. Tucker's astonishment when a shot shattered the dawn was etched in his face as he pitched to the earth.

Buck Dawson blew wisps of gunsmoke from the barrel of his revolver. "I never have liked pushy salesmen much."

To the north, on the road, hooves drummed, accoutrements rattled, and a commanding voice bellowed for a patrol to halt.

"Is that what I think it is?" Gwen eagerly asked.

Fargo wearily nodded. Against all odds, and the treachery of one of their own, they had survived. The nightmare was over. Now he could finally get on with his life. Or could he?

Melissa Starr and Gwen Pearson were advancing, hands on their hips and wrath crackling on their brows. "We have a bone to pick with you, mister," the redhead declared.

Fargo hoped the cavalry would hurry.

LOOKING FORWARD!
The following is the opening
section from the next novel in the exciting
***Trailsman* series from Signet:**

THE TRAILSMAN #209
TIMBER TERROR

Montana, 1861, the logging country just north of the
Sapphire Mountains where trees were not the only thing
cut down and the two-legged timberwolves were worse
than the four-legged kind . . .

"Coming events cast their shadows before them."

The big man with the lake blue eyes uttered the phrase as he guided the magnificent Ovaro between two towering Ponderosa pines, his voice colored with wry amusement. Written by a man named Joseph Campbell, the phrase had stayed with Skye Fargo ever since he'd first read it. It had proven itself to be true all too often but always when hindsight had given the shadows form and meaning, and everyone knew that hindsight was always too late to be of practical help. Shadows, Fargo reflected, were hard to interpret, even for a trailsman.

His lake blue eyes narrowed as they swept the rugged terrain. Certainly the high-mountain country of north Montana held plenty of its own shadows. Named Land of the Mountains by the Spanish conquistadors, it was a land that offered pleasure and hardship, beauty and danger, in equal measure. As he rode from the north, the Sapphire Mountains in front of him, the Bitterroot Range rising in the distance on his right, he wondered if Abbey had been one of those events that cast their shadows. It had to be a good shadow she cast, benign and filled with pleasure memories. Her eager passion, unrestricted ecstasy and ample breasts could cast nothing else. He had made the long detour into the north Montana high country, hoping she still ran the small sheep ranch with her brother. He discovered that she did and together they turned the clock back to old pleasures with new urgency.

It had been almost a week he'd spent with Abbey and he smiled as he rode, a parade of intimacies and memories surrounding him. He'd been surprised at how little things he'd thought forgotten leaped up at once as though they'd simply been waiting for a time to wake. Abbey's nipples were two of those memories, always so very small on her ample breasts, as though they really ought to belong to a very young, very small girl. But their tiny mounds were fountains of sensitivity, rising at once, reaching upward to give and be given. It had always been that way with Abbey and time hadn't changed that at all. The week that followed had been all he could have hoped for, the feeling mutual, she acknowledged when the week drew to an end. "You have to go," she said as she lay exhausted beside him, her slightly chunky body quivering with spent passion. "I'm not getting any of my work done. All my chores are piling up. Or stay with me always," she added. "And I know you won't do that."

He didn't answer and they both knew he had. She'd clung to him before he left after breakfast, leaving the only regret they shared. Abbey rode with him, a welcome companion if only in his thoughts. Shadows. He grunted. If they were being cast by coming events they could only be good ones.

Shaking off idle thoughts, he steered the Ovaro down a deer trail as he scanned the land. He always felt small riding this land. The tremendous Douglas firs, Engelman spruce, ponderosa pines, the giant sequoias and the red cedar were giants to make anything and anyone feel small. This was logging country, evidence almost anywhere he looked, the stumps of fallen trees, the broken pieces of a bucking saw, the long hafts of a splintered falling ax and the ubiquitous hooked oilcans left lying on the forest floor.

But mostly, the land was imprinted by the thousands of logs that floated down every river, tributary, lake, and waterway. Still other logs were seen stored in big ponds behind splash dams, built for the purpose, waiting for the moment when the spill gate of the dam was pulled away and the cascade of logs sent hurtling down to the river or lake. Riding through logging country always gave him a mixed feeling, Fargo acknowledged. There was a violation here, the power and beauty of nature being destroyed by man's uncaring greed. Someday a better way of using the timber would be found than the unchecked logging practiced now, he told himself. There had to be if the treasure of the great forests were to be renewed for others. But now there was a headlong selfishness, a dark spirit of destruction that had to affect the destroyers as well as the destroyed. These loggers were a breed unto themselves, he knew, personally brave and foolhardy, the lumberjacks simply crude and unthinking, their bosses adding greed and contempt to their legacy.

Fargo turned the Ovaro along the edge of a narrow river, into the open sun that made the horse's jet black fore- and hindquarters glisten, its pure white midsection gleam. Fallen logs all but filled the narrow river, moving faster than they seemed to move from a distance, no room between them as one pushed against the other. Suddenly his eyes rested on a figure almost in the center of the logs. The man lay facedown, his legs hanging into the water, caught between logs, the one he clung to and the one that held him pinned against it. Fargo sent the pinto into a canter, down a steep bank that deposited him at the water's edge. He peered across the carpet of logs that moved down the river. Though still traveling slowly, they were gathering speed as they moved into the center of the river, jostling each other with increasing force.

Fargo pulled the pinto to a halt and swung from the saddle, leaping onto the nearest logs that drifted past him. Landing on both feet simultaneously, he felt the logs instantly move under his weight. Though the movement was slight, it was enough to send some of the logs immediately climbing over others. Though he didn't wear the cleated, caulked logger's boots, he began to make his way across the logs, leaping lightly from one to the other. But the logs moved, unexpectedly, some sinking down, others shifting away, and he found each step becoming a tricky little dance with the creak and scrape of logs the only rhythm. But his eyes went to the still figure as he became more convinced the man would be crushed as soon as the logs that held him began to gather speed when they reached midriver.

Leaping forward more recklessly, Fargo neared the figure, finally halting on the log that trapped the man's legs. Dropping down, Fargo used both feet and all the strength of his powerful leg muscles to push against the next log. It moved, even with the pressure of other logs against it, opening up enough for him to reach out and swing the man's legs out of the water and onto the log on which he lay. Straightening up, Fargo stepped onto the log where the man lay. He knelt down on one knee to turn the man onto his back. He felt the frown dig into his brow as the figure wouldn't turn. Leaning closer, he tried again, then saw the two big tenpenny nails that had been driven into the log. Ropes ran from the nails around the man's wrists.

The frown digging deeper, Fargo stared at the figure. The

man hadn't fallen and been trapped by the crush of adjoining logs. He'd been nailed to the log and sent out into the river with the mass of other logs. The terrible truth speared into Fargo. The man had been nailed to the log to be crushed to death when the logs gathered speed and climbed over each other. But death hadn't waited to claim him, perhaps mercifully so, Fargo saw. The logs that had trapped his legs had also taken life from him, probably by sheer loss of blood. Sitting back on his haunches, his eyes riveted on the lifeless figure, thoughts whirled inside him. If the man had been crushed by other logs, the wrists ropes would have been torn away. Had it been a clever way to hide a killing? Or had he been put there not to hide anything but to be an example?

Did it much matter? He asked himself. It was a cold-blooded killing. The reasons wouldn't change that. They'd only put a face on it, nothing more. He'd let others struggle with that, in their own way, in their own time. He was but passing by. The bitter taste stayed in his mouth as he rose to his feet and began to hop his way across the logs, a treacherous, shifting floor. Suddenly a huge redwood rose up and drove itself forward over another log and straight at him with thunderous speed. He spun, half leaped, half dived, and landed on a nearby log, then jumped onto another and continued to find his way over the logs. Finally, with a long jump, his feet hit the soft earth of the shoreline and he heard his own breath escape him.

Turning, he watched the logs gathering speed as they went by and he slowly walked back to where the Ovaro waited. The questions clung to him as he pulled himself onto the horse and rode up the embankment and away from the waterway. He rode south again, refusing to dwell on what he'd seen, though other logs in other waterways refused to let him forget. He was passing through, he reminded himself again, and he'd let it stay that way. Moving through the thick forests of red cedar and lodgepole pine, he heard the distant sounds of logging operations, the crash of the huge trees that reverberated for miles, the sounds of big, double-handled bucksaws, and the sharp crack of broadaxes. The sounds faded away as he rode deeper into untouched, virgin timberland, and as dusk began to slide into the day, he slowed to a halt.

He listened, his head inclined to one side, and his eyes scanning the forest from beneath the frown that had again come to his forehead. He sat very still, his wild-creature hearing picking up the sounds. They had intruded on him since he'd entered the virgin forest. This time it was the whir of wings taking flight, an entire charm of goldfinches with their black foreheads and black wings filling the sky. Before that it had been a herd of black-tailed deer, all fleeing through the forest at once, startled and fearful of an alien presence. Before that there had been the tremendous racket of a murder of crows, the kind only set off when they were unexpectedly disturbed. Crows, being what they are, didn't just fly away as most birds would. They stayed, swooped in huge groups, and angrily cawed and protested, aggressively showing their displeasure. Finally they had calmed down. But before that there had been the unmistakable rustling sound of grouse taking wing almost straight up.

It had all been a good distance behind him yet it had persisted, one sound after the other, each a message to those who could understand. He had ridden casually and made no effort to cover his tracks, but he was becoming convinced that either someone was following and searching out trailmarks, or happened to be riding along the same paths. Fargo grunted at the last thought. He never dismissed coincidence. He just didn't put much store in them. As night supplanted dusk, he swung from the Ovaro and led the horse into a dense thicket of hackberry with plenty of wild geranium to soften the land and welcome a bedroll. He ate cold beef jerky, certain that darkness had put a stop to anyone tracking him. Then he lay down and listened to the night sounds, the clatter of scarab beetles, the buzz of insects, the soft swoosh of bats, and the chatter of kit foxes, until finally he slept.

When morning came he found a stream, washed, and rode on until the trees thinned out enough to leave patches of open land. He stopped, dismounted, and used his boots to scrape marks on the ground, then pressed a circle in the grass. He used his canteen to damp down the grass inside the circle he'd scraped. He finished, added a few more meaningless marks, and smiled. Even he wouldn't know what to make of them. Taking the Ovaro behind a cluster of cottonwoods, he sat down against the furrowed, pale bark and waited. The sun had reached the noon sky when he heard the horse approaching in clustered, hesitant steps, the rider pausing often to search the ground.

Fargo was on his feet behind the tree trunk when the horse pushed into sight, a dark brown gelding, the rider on it no more than eighteen years old, he guessed, as he took in the young man's smooth cheeks and full, unruly black hair. The youth halted, dismounted, and knelt down beside the markings on the ground. Fargo watched the frown of consternation gather on his forehead as he studied the markings. "Real confusing, isn't it, junior?" Fargo said as he stepped from behind the tree. "What do you make of it?" Startled, the young man straightened up and spun, one hand moving toward the gun at his hip. "I wouldn't do that, junior," Fargo said quietly. The youth's hand dropped to his side and his eyes went to the marks on the ground.

"You make these?" he asked.

Fargo smiled as he nodded. "Figured they'd give you something to wonder about," he said.

"They did. I'd have spent hours trying to figure them out. Why didn't you go on?" the youth asked.

"Curiosity," Fargo said. "You've been following me."

"Been following tracks, hoping," the young man said.

"Hoping what?" Fargo queried.

"That you'd be Skye Fargo," the youth said.

"What made you figure I might be?" Fargo asked.

"Heard you were staying at Abbey Carson's. I stopped there. She told me you'd gone on due south. I followed. Yours were the only single rider tracks I came onto."

"If I was Skye Fargo, what then?"

"There's somebody wants to see you. I was sent to find you," the young man said.

"Who, why, and what for?" Fargo asked.

The youth started to answer but he had only opened his lips when the shot rang out, the heavy crack of a rifle. Fargo saw the young man's unruly black hair bounce in all directions as the bullet smashed into him. Clutching his side with a groan, he fell as another shot rang out, followed by more. Fargo dived and hit the ground as he saw the riders racing into sight. Six, he counted automatically. They were still concentrating their fire on the young man stretched out on the ground but Fargo rolled and flung himself into the trees as bullets began to kick up dirt inches from him. The brush closing over him, he yanked the Colt from its holster as he saw the attackers start to come after him. Two led the charge and Fargo aimed and fired, and the two men dropped from their horses as if they'd both been pulled off by one invisible rope. The other four immediately swerved into tree cover and Fargo took the moment to retreat behind the trunk of a big cottonwood.

He heard the young man on the ground moan and heard the four riders dismount and start to come after him on foot, staying in the trees. They were overeager hired guns, he saw, and they stayed too close together as they moved toward him. He raised the Colt, steadied the gun against the tree trunk, and let one of the figures move into sight, another at his heels. Both were in a half crouch but moving too quickly, again their overeager amateurism obvious. The Colt barked twice, the second shot only a half-inch away from the first, and both figures went down at once. Fargo waited and heard the other two halt and crouch. They were suddenly uncertain, fear gripping them in its paralyzing hold. His ears picked up the sound of their feet sliding backward, and then suddenly turning to run. He shifted position to the other side of the tree trunk, his gaze fixed on the spot where they had ridden into the trees.

He had only seconds to wait when the two horses burst from the trees, racing over the open ground to reach the thick tree cover from which they'd appeared. Fargo had time for only one shot, chose the rider at the right, and fired. The man fell forward, hit the saddle horn, and the motion of the galloping horse did the rest, tossing him into the air to hit the ground with a resounding thud and lie still. The last rider raced on, vanishing into the trees. Fargo listened to the sound of his horse as it fled. Holstering the Colt, Fargo ran forward to the young man and knelt down beside the red-stained figure. He was still breathing. Grimacing, Fargo took in the extent of the wounds that soaked the youth's clothes, at least four bullets, he saw. The youth managed to lift his head a few inches from the ground. "Easy, take it easy," Fargo murmured.

"Tillman . . . Darlene Tillman . . . waiting for you," the young man managed to gasp. "Important . . . go see her." The effort took the last of his strength, words ending with a final gasp and Fargo leaned back as he softly cursed. He rose after a moment and walked to where the other figures littered the ground. He examined each one and found nothing to help him. But someone had sent them to find the young man and stop him before he could deliver his message. They had almost succeeded, Fargo grunted angrily. Almost. His eyes went to the young, slender figure. The youth had given his life in his assignment. *Somebody better have a good explanation,* Fargo thought as he went to the youth's horse, drew a blanket from the saddlebag, and wrapped it around the silent, stained figure.

He lifted the youth, laid him across his saddle, and walked to the Ovaro. Holding the reins of the brown gelding in one hand, Fargo slowly started to ride on south. He'd no way of knowing if south was the way to go and hoped he'd find somebody who might help. As he rode, he tried to piece together the few bits and pieces of information he had. The young man had visited Abbey looking for him. That meant he had to have first visited Ed Stanford up near Ninepipe. Ed was the only one who knew he was going to visit Abbey, Fargo recalled. They'd spent a few days talking after he'd broken the trail from Idaho Territory for Ed. But Ed wasn't the only one who knew about his coming to Montana. Ed had told enough others that he'd hired Skye Fargo to break a trail for him.

So finding he had visited Abbey was explainable. Then the youth had followed south, picked up the trail, and met his death because of it. A Darlene Tillman had hired him, he'd muttered with his last breath. Not much to go on but it would be enough. Fargo had found trails with slimmer leads. He felt a bitterness inside him, first at what he'd witnessed, and then at being plunged into something he knew absolutely nothing about. The young man had been a total stranger and yet now he was suddenly no stranger at all. He was suddenly someone with whom Fargo had become involved. That imposition angered him, Fargo realized. He certainly had no responsibility for the youth's death, yet a kind of oblique responsibility had been thrust upon him.

Damn, Fargo swore as he found himself thinking about coming events that cast their shadows before them. If he had not stayed the glorious week with Abbey, he would have been long gone from this north Montana country. If he hadn't told Ed Stanford he was going to visit Abbey, the man wouldn't have been able to tell the youth. There'd have been no one to trail him, to pursue him with still undelivered messages. Coming events did cast their shadows, but you could only understand them after they'd been cast.

What shadows was he riding into now, Fargo wondered as he moved past a lake half filled with logs, a big splash dam holding back hundreds of other logs. Perhaps he'd be wise to let the brown gelding behind him find its own way, he pondered. But he wouldn't, he knew. The young man wrapped in the blanket behind him deserved to have his message delivered. Everybody deserved some kind of obituary.